Continuous Blinking:
Critical Thinking Stories and Questions for Clever and Determined Young Thinkers

Andrew Lee

London Amazon KDP 2023

Continuous Blinking:
Critical Thinking Stories and Questions for Clever and
Determined Young Thinkers

First published by KDP 2023
Copyright © Andrew Lee (2023)
KDP ISBN: 9798863187761

All correspondence should be directed to the author at draklee@mac.com

Cover design by Andrew Lee
Printed by Amazon KDP Print

I lovingly dedicate this book to my parents,
who have both sadly moved on,
but some of their stories, experiences and
turns of phrase get the occasional cameo in
Continuous Blinking.

Table of Contents

Introduction..7

Acknowledgements & Preamble 10

For Readers of this Book...12

1 Millfield Library...15

2 Gravity Hiccups 21

3 The Dangers of Words... 25

4 The Trees... 29

5 Anstead: The Vandal of History.. 32

6 Florian, for want of a better name 36

7 Renata 41

8 The World Department Store 47

9 Ermonza.. 54

10 Mrs McCulvert lived alone 62

11 André and the Toaster 71

12 Inevitability 79

13 Uncertainty... 93

14 A Dog's Day 97

15 Butterfly Wings...111

A whole bunch of things to think about… 118

1 Millfield Library... 119

2 Gravity Hiccups 121

3 The Dangers of Words.. 123

4 The Trees... 125

5 Anstead 127

6 Florian, for want of a better name 129

7 Renata 131

8 The World Department Store 133

9 Ermonza 136

10 Mrs McCulvert Lived Alone 139

11 André and the Toaster 143

12 Inevitability 146

13 Uncertainty 148

14 A Dog's Day 150

15 Butterfly Wings...153

Your mind is a palace.

Frank McCourt, Angela's Ashes

Introduction

As education becomes increasingly driven by state curricula focused on educating young people to be employable, schools find themselves increasingly providing *know how* rather than *know why*. Despite educational objectives which build such questions into their treatment of the subject, *know why*, at least in part, comes from reflection and contemplation, something that is being squeezed out of the curriculum because of a lack of time and perhaps due to a change in pedagogical currency.

Yet the marginalisation of 'space-to-think-in' is a dangerous development, especially as the information smorgasbord, as it is purveyed today through multimedia, internet and even the now 'old hat' video resources, means that available information is potentially unreliable, biased or just plain wrong. Artificial 'Intelligence' risks us going down another such rabbit hole especially as its sources become more unreliable and in-bred. Fake and biased news leads to false information, misunderstanding, and flawed reasoning. Indeed, it is at this very moment with the proliferation of information kiosks, that the student must become pointedly discerning and ethically robust in order to evaluate information in terms of assessing bias, sourcing, ethical stance, and ownership. Moreover, the tendency for a pupil to think it reasonable to find an answer (on the internet or via Chat GPT) rather than to write an answer for themselves begs the question about intellectual property and the integrity of authorship.

Where information is at their fingertips, many assume that purveying information is the same as creating or synthesising it. Whilst some of these imperatives are not entirely new, with on-going leaps in technology, the sheer scale and penetration of modern IT means that the skills of independent and clear thinking will be more and more important to the lives of the individual. In short, we need people who can think, question, and understand.

Yet young people also need a sense of wonder - the real crux of education. There are dark dangers in alienating our young from wonder, the opportunity to ask questions about those things that are often taken for granted.

In the past, childhood extended right into the teens, but information increasingly ages the young by giving them knowledge. Knowing how to manage that knowledge is essential. The swelling of the wider availability of knowledge is not matched by the wisdom that young people would once develop through stories and moments of reflection and discovery found in the play of unstructured time.

A sense of wonder prepared to transgress the taken-for-granted world of the child needs to be fostered if they are to adeptly navigate our modern world. Otherwise, we are in danger of pumping, by means of the informated society, our offspring full of knowledge and the capacity to find knowledge, without having the faculties of reason, imagination, or question. Where information becomes increasingly plentiful and indeed variable in quality, even if plausible in format, the social context of our young needs to provide not only avenues of discourse, but a desire and a capacity for it. As young people increasingly, if not unexpectedly, become disenchanted with politics, developing a willingness and ability to engage in debate, and to think hard, creatively and well, will be necessary to drive change.

This book begins to unlock the important and to some degree nascent talents and propensities in young people to question the right-way-roundedness of the world. Alan Alder, the famous American actor, in the popular English radio programme *Desert Island Discs*, said that having a schizophrenic mother made him constantly aware of the need to test reality as it was purveyed to him. Was what his mother said to him every morning, even within the bounds of possibility? Is the reality of our own world within the bounds of possibility or totally untenable?

Traditionally the child grapples with the reality of the adult world with the onset of puberty. As this process comes earlier and earlier, it is important for our young people to be equipped with more than just the information and disinformation that makes up the world. This book is a roller coaster ride through magnifying glasses, time machines and worlds of topsy turvy. Like the vision of the Surrealists, moments of the macabre make us question those things which we hold true - not necessarily to disprove them, but just to shake the foundations so that we can test whether they be safe or to confirm suspicions that they may actually be ill-founded.

Andrew Lee
November 2023

Acknowledgements & Preamble

These stories were written some years ago when I was teaching at my own prep school, to which I had returned to teach for a short while. I had been asked to teach a weekly lesson on Critical Thinking. A critical thinker was something that I always considered myself to be, and certainly when teaching at Oxford, having undergraduates defend their essays every week, critical thinking was a skill I honed over many years.

In any case, I was handed a book of short stories from which to teach Critical Thinking. I detested that book! After trying to make it work, I hatched a plan. My class had PE before my Critical Thinking lesson and I was free during the morning - so I had some time up my sleeve, and so every week I would write a story for the class. I didn't tell them I had written the stories, but some became a little suspicious as I would often include fragments in the stories that were eerily pertinent to that week's events. This is the joy of story-telling. These stories became *Continuous Blinking*.

Firstly, I owe my thanks, to those pupils who were the proving ground for my stories. I wonder if any of them remember?

Secondly, I owe enormous gratitude to Dr Phil West who was Head of Religious Studies at Westminster Under School, in London, when I was on the staff there as Head of Year and Head of Geography. Dr West has published a swag of wonderful and highly successful critical thinking stories himself, and he encouraged me to publish mine.

Thirdly, thanks to Helene Jones, who runs Nimble Minds, and teaches Critical Thinking at Wetherby Prep School. I gave her my stories which she thought were great, and who kindly asked whether she could use them in her courses, which she currently does. She also encouraged me to publish the stories.

Fourthly to Elizabeth Harre, Head of Strings at Radley College, who I have known for many years. Having many strings to her bow, she is also a proof-reader. She kindly proofread my manuscript.

Images throughout the book were generated with the assistance of AI; and the handshake image was from Freepik.com. All images generated on 7 August 2023. The cover was designed by me; and I own the copyright to all images therein.

For Readers of this Book

I wrote these stories for children who I was teaching. I wanted to write stories that made them think. I have spent a lot of time teaching, but I have also spent a lot of time thinking and reading.

When I was at university one of the subjects I studied was Philosophy. (Philosophy is about what it means to be human, how we fit into the world and relate to its people.)

I took the course because they said it had 'no exams.' I thought this was the course for me! But they tricked me. Not because there were exams, there were not; but because they wanted to get me to study philosophy because they knew I would enjoy it; and I did.

We can live our lives without thinking about things, but what kind of life is that? It suits many people, but not me. Philosophy faces the difficult and unsolved problems of life; and with all of what is happening with climate change, wars, Artificial Intelligence, and political turmoil, we need to keep thinking. It is our only hope. We must do things as well, but we need to know what we're doing and why.

It is one thing to have the know-how, but the people who make decisions will need to know the know-why and the know what-for, and to have thought about what might happen if we make a particular decision or do a particular thing. We all need to keep thinking about what the right things to do are.

These stories are a little odd, but they are deliberately like this, so that you think about things a little differently. This is your challenge. Good luck.

Keep up to date with Continuous Blinking by visiting continuousblinking.com

Click on the continuousblinking button.

1 Millfield Library

This story is about the way that history becomes distorted and the way that truth and fiction are often mixed.

Mrs Jacques was the librarian of Millfield Library. She had always been a librarian, or so it seemed. No one in the town could ever remember her ever not being the librarian, and some people in the village were quite old. Oddly enough, Mrs Jacques never seemed to look older one day or year to the next. Moreover, she was a woman whose age was hard to estimate; she could have been thirty, or fifty or perhaps even older … or younger. Although this seemed odd, she was such an efficient librarian and had such great knowledge that no one dared ever question her about the fact she never seemed to get older, or ever seemed to be any particular age.

The library was spotless - it was like a hospital of knowledge. All day long Mrs Jacques would be sorting books, organising information. She was a sort of wizard of everything that was known, or perhaps a guardian of the citadel of truth. People would sometimes come by and ask things like, "What is the highest mountain in Chile?" "Who was the first person to climb the Inaccessible Pinnacle?" and so on. She always, *always* knew the answers to the questions that she was asked.

Not once did she ever need to open one of the books she so carefully looked after and catalogued. One never knew whether she had read all the books, or whether she didn't need to read them because she had known what was in the books already.

There was, however, one third thing that was odd about the Millfield Municipal Library - this was the catalogue - or perhaps more accurately, the way that the books were organised. In a common library all the fiction books are in one area of the library and all the non-fiction books in another area of the library. In such a library fact and fiction never meet, often even being kept in separate rooms. It is as if librarians everywhere held fears that the non-fiction collection may pollute the fiction or perhaps more dangerously, that fiction may infect non-fiction.

However, Mrs Jacques seemed to have no such fears, in fact she positively encouraged the mixture. She placed all the books together so that in her library Science was with Science Fiction, and History was with Historical Novels. It was a rather odd way to run a library, but no one ever disagreed or even commented on it because Mrs Jacques ran such a good library.

That is until Wednesday 6th August, when a little boy called André came into the library and was so astounded by the way the books were kept, that he stormed right up to the librarian and said, "What a disgraceful mess."

Now one would have expected Mrs Jacques to be dumbfounded, but instead she looked at André, whom she had never seen before, and said, "I knew this would happen sooner or later."

"How can you possibly run a library like this - with books all mixed up? It's not proper!" protested André who was an arrogant little squirt.

"André," said Mrs Jacques knowingly, and shocking her protagonist because he had not yet given her his name, "let me explain. But first," said Mrs Jacques, "I want to ask you a question. What is so special about today?"

André looked at her disdainfully, expressing to her with his eyes that he did not care for this sort of game, but also that he would humour her, and said, "Nothing much, it's a Wednesday; in August..."

"Stop there," said Mrs Jacques, "today is in fact a boundary. What happens now is the present, what happened only just then when you came in the door is the past, and what will happen in a moment's time is the future."

"So what?" said a frustratingly bored André.

"So," said Mrs Jacques, "What happens right now turns from fact into fiction. Before our very eyes we witness the future turn into the now and then into fiction."

"No it doesn't," screeched André thinking that the librarian was a silly old bat, "things that happen now don't turn into fiction, they turn into history."

"Well d-e-a-r boy," said Mrs Jacques in a patronising tone, "what is history if it is not fiction?"

"It is non-fiction," said André in a self-satisfied sort of way.

"Balderdash," said Mrs Jacques, "poppycock and flapdoodle. When the present becomes the past it becomes a story. You see André it is never possible to tell the whole truth; truth always becomes distorted. Who is to say that a history book tells the truth? No one can really know the truth once something has happened; all there is, is a sum of the stories that one person can tell another and write down - if you're lucky. His story ('his' story, or 'her' story for the women who made history) is only a series of stories with lots and lots left out. Who are we to judge whether what was left out was really the important bit or not?

History changes too. If you read history books today, they disagree with history books that were written fifty years ago. Human beings make up history, and it changes! How can I put such things in the non-fiction section and sleep well at night André? How can I?"

André was reluctantly beginning to get the point.

"But André, more importantly, sometimes there is more truth in stories, real stories, stories by Shakespeare, by Tolstoy and Joyce, even in Charlie Brown; André, stuff you would have me put in the fiction section of the library."

"But how can that possibly be true Mrs Jacques?" asked André, wanting to surprise her by also knowing her name.

"Well André," said the librarian who knew that André had seen her name glued to the front desk, "truth lies in the strangest places. Truth can be found in stories of courage and determination when the *flavour* of the past is not only more important but also more accurately painted by writers than politicians and historians who often have an interest in mistreating the truth. Truth can be found in humour, in jokes and in art."

"I see," said André, "thank you Mrs Jacques, I must go home to my mother now. She is expecting me for tea. But tell me first before I go, is it easy to find a book in this library?"

"No," said Mrs Jacques, "it's virtually impossible."

2 Gravity Hiccups

Whilst seemingly about lapses in gravity, this story challenges the ever presence of things which are taken for granted and asks what would happen if the principles on which one always relied, were no longer to be relied on. The narrative is in the form of an unfinished story.

It was Tuesday. I hated Tuesdays. This Tuesday was the day when the Science Council announced what advances had been made in the scientific community that week. The press would all be there, and we would have to sit through a lot of babble about genetic streaming and solar storm tangents. Nothing ever occurred which had importance now; most things had been discovered except for a cure for the common cold; that continued to stump them.

I went into the auditorium to listen to Professor Blunden. He stood up at the dais and looked remarkably and uncharacteristically stern. What was it to be this week? The discovery of a synthetic rat enzyme, the announcement of a new cure for the disease corn gets when grown upside down in Arctic conditions, or a cure for sheep diarrhoea? The professor began.

"An important and grave discovery has been made," he said.

"What else is new?" I thought.

"The Science Council has, after careful research, found that owing to the growing anthropocentric carbon dioxide in the atmosphere, which began in the Nineteenth Century with the burning of fossil fuels in a process called the Industrial Revolution, the earth has been developing a problem with its gravitational field. It seems that because of the melting of the ice caps, there is less mass at the North and South Poles than has ever been the case in the known past. This has caused a shift in the centre of gravity of the earth and the core of our planet is being fundamentally changed. It seems that in the next ten years or so humankind will have to cope with what the Council has termed, 'gravity hiccups.'"

All of a sudden there was a great murmur from the press. Cameras rolled, flashes went off and press agents stood up and began to yell questions. The atmosphere in the room became heated and reporters began to yell out questions at the professor. A security guard stood up - he was about seven foot tall. Suddenly, all the press sat down and shut up.

"Ladies and gentlemen, let me continue," said the professor in a voice meant to calm the journalists down, "It seems that without warning, in the next ten years we will begin to see these gravitational hiccups more and more often. These hiccups will last for around twenty seconds per day. For around twenty seconds a day, as the gravitational centre of the earth shifts, gravity will not function. Then following the event, gravity will be restored. Ladies and gentlemen, this is an announcement of very great importance. This is also a challenge, a challenge to the scientific and engineering community to keep us safe - you see we need to plan for this contingency well in advance if we are to protect ourselves from great loss of life. I know you will all have a lot of questions, and so I ask for questions from the floor."

Tom Davies stood up. Tom was the reader of the 9 o'clock news and perhaps the country's most experienced journalist. "Professor," he asked, "does this mean that everyone will just float for twenty seconds a day?"

The professor replied, "That's right Tom, hard as it may be to believe, everything would, or could float. Thankfully the gravity loss will not normally affect the soil and ground cover because it is not moving and is largely held together by surface tension, but soil and loose particles could float, especially if any force is exerted on them. Buildings too should be safe because they are connected by strong foundations, though loose-fitting items may float away. At the moment we are not sure of the details."

"Professor, this is a very serious suggestion, are you sure that this is likely to happen? How can we…"

The professor interjected, "Tom there is nothing the Science Council is surer of, and I could not make this public statement if we were in any way uncertain. We cannot tell the exact duration of the hiccups or exactly when they will begin, but they're coming all right. Research has been in progress during the last eighteen months and every single test proves without a doubt that this is what we are to expect."

3 The Dangers of Words

This story is about the way that words and messages can sometimes be contradictory. It promotes the need to be critical about what is read. The story suggests that just because something is written does not mean it is right.

LIAR

Mitchell always walked home the same way from school. He would go across the brook, down the lane, past the dairy farm and down into the valley where his mother's house was. His father had died many years ago and he and his mother lived alone in a small but comfortable house by the side of a river called the Esker. They were not rich, but they also were not poor - they had what they needed and not much more. Every year they went on holiday and every now and then they went off for special treats. Mitchell's mother worked 'doing the books' at the local bakery, and one thing was for certain, there was always fresh bread on the table.

Mitchell was eleven and was getting to the stage, after three years of being somewhat bored with the way that he walked home, of deciding to take a different route. By the windmill on the hill there was a little track that went past where the hang gliders would take off and skirted around Horace Hill to the banks of the Esker where he could wander home. It was a longer way home, but at least it wasn't quite so boring, and from time to time he would catch a glimpse of a hang glider soaring through the sky.

Along the way he passed a house, which he had never noticed before. It was a very old house, even though to him it was quite new. The funny thing about it was that it seemed to have no door, only windows. On his way home he would walk around the house in the hope of finding the door, or in the hope that one would miraculously reveal itself to him. Yet as much as he would try to find the door, he never came across it. No one ever seemed to come in or go out and there was no sign of the house being inhabited - which for a house without a door was perhaps hardly surprising.

In any case in Mitchell's wanderings around the house, he came to notice that there was a sign in one of the windows. This he thought strange because as far as he could see there would never be anyone around to read it. He went over to see what it said. It said, "Do not read this sign."

Mitchell thought this a peculiar sign, much as you would expect an eleven-year-old boy might and he continued his journey home. Now Mitchell wasn't one normally to spend too much time thinking about things, but he did think about this one. "What could it mean?" he thought to himself.

The sign said one thing, but it seemed to contradict itself. To know what the sign said, you needed to disobey it. The sign made you disobey it. It was as if the sign made you commit a crime. It was less a message and more a trick pretending to be a sign. He wondered whether anything else happened in this way. Are there things that seem to be one thing but are in fact quite something else? He wondered.

When he got home another strange thing happened. When he got to the door of his house and began to wipe his feet, for it had been muddy along the Esker, he noticed that there seemed to be writing on the doormat. He stood back, in shock, at least at first, and tried to read what was written on it. It said, "The statement on the other side of this mat is false." "How odd," thought Mitchell, and he picked up the mat to see what was written on the other side. "The statement on the other side of the mat is true," was written underneath the mat.

If the statement on the back of the mat is false, as it said on the front, then this would mean that the statement on the front was false as well, thought Mitchell. If the statement on the front were false, then the statement on the back would need to be true.

"How odd," thought Mitchell, as he went inside to have his biscuits and milk.

4 The Trees

A story about freedom of expression, eccentricity, and difference.

Jack was fascinated by trees. From the day he was born and was put in his cot he gazed out of the conservatory window up into the very umbrella of leaves that shaded him from the beaming sun. The trees swayed and made patterns on the floor and dappled him with light. In that conservatory listening to the symphony of leaves on blustery days he began his lifelong friendship with the trees, the great foundations of the sky.

As a boy he took up carpentry and learnt not only to respect the timber that he used, but to shape and sculpt it. He admired the springiness of the yew, the fragrance of the elm bark, and the foliage of the plane tree. He paid attention to what the trees did and how they swayed, and he wondered about the wood as the trees yielded to the winds and breezes.

Now Jack was a gentle lad, a boy of great sensitivity. He loved the trees and he felt that the trees which he came across, in some way, looked after him. On walks in the countryside, he found himself comforted by them. Yet he was sad because some of the trees rarely flowered. Although they were perpetually there, to Jack they seemed somewhat sad, somewhat vulnerable. They played their role in protecting him, but in just one night they may be knocked over by winds or storms. There was a vulnerability in the trees, one that he deeply cherished. For Jack the trees were magnificent, but they were also sad and tragic.

Of all the trees he knew of, he held most respect for the dipterocarps of Borneo. They spent long stretches of time hiding themselves. Jack loved the dipterocarps because they only flowered once every hundred and fifty years or so. They resisted telling their secrets to anyone, so rarely was the beauty of their flowers ever seen. Even when they bloomed, they told no one, and those who found out, those who stumbled upon this secret moment, those who happened on the tree in the moment when it was revealed, were sentenced to death. They *would* die before the tree would reveal itself again and certainly before they could tell others of their beauty - others who may lie awake through the nights in the hope of seeing this secret moment. The tree lived too long to waste its secrets on mortal man.

Yet, the dipterocarp had many varieties but flowered so infrequently that it disguised itself as any other dipterocarp. These trees were masters of camouflage -

they had found the perfect hiding spot - to dwell amongst themselves secretly. Each species dwelt there indistinguishable from any of the other trees until they chose a moment to be different. Even scientists were unable to tell the dipterocarps apart - at least until they flowered. And flower they never did, seemingly, certainly not for the scientists. When, secretly, they chose to flower, they flowered only to their own species and deep in the impenetrable jungle. Their moment was fleeting, momentary, ephemeral - only they knew it. Only they witnessed the dance of their souls.

Jack lived a peaceful life amongst the trees deep in the bush. There he made ornaments and watched as the forest grew around him. Yet the trees around him never showed him their secret, and nor did they witness the dancing of Jack's soul for, because just like the trees that he loved, Jack would not dance if he had no audience - and throughout Jack's life he never found another who loved trees as much as he did - and so, except for being with the trees, he lived and died alone.

5 Anstead: The Vandal of History

This story explores the way that history is constructed and the dangers of the taken-for-grantedness of time.

Anstead thrived on mischief. Anstead's mischief was not the mischief of naughtiness in the back garden, normally expected of children, but the mischief that drives criminals and those who just like to cause trouble. Yet Anstead's reasoning, whilst it could have been evil, was in fact a peculiar type of kindness, because his mischief was a mischief of vandalism and was purely intended as an irritant to make strong those who sought to fix the damage done. Anstead's work was like that of a computer hacker who tried to break into computers, in the hope that those who looked after the computer system would learn to protect it.

Anstead was a vandal, quite unlike any other, for the thing that Anstead vandalised was time - or history to be exact. Anstead sailed across time planting lies. He sprinkled them around history like fairies sprinkle wanderlust. He traipsed around, in every corner of history, and he spread lies. Sometimes he would deposit small subtle lies that may never be detected and sometimes he would land great whoppers of lies that would stand out for all to laugh at. Anstead played in the darkness and danced his way through history to make sure that things just didn't make sense. He placed animals in places where they could not have been - just to upset the scientists when they uncovered fossils in millions of years' time. He put iron in the campfires of Neanderthals even before iron could have been invented. He put glass where there could be no glass, he put documents which could not have been discovered - it is even rumoured that it was he who had hidden the Dead Sea scrolls.

What a life Anstead led, how he enjoyed watching the officials in suits and scientists in white lab coats scratch their heads in disbelief just when they finally thought they had it, go mad when they discovered something different, something that meant that all their research must be wrong. How he laughed when the professors and the researchers hid their findings because they couldn't believe or explain what they had found; how he giggled when famous archaeologists failed to explain things that they had dug up and just put the most important thing they had found somewhere on the shelf in the backroom. Anstead knew that the dusty old skull lying in a box which read Peak Freans Biscuits should have been responsible for dispelling every modern idea about the history of man. How funny that it should be in a biscuit box, with its teeth rattling every time the caretaker's dog ran past.

What pathetic creatures, thought Anstead, when he watched them as he passed. One of Anstead's greatest successes was the Institute of Apichu Culture in Middle Peru. By carefully placing a few odd things together, where the archaeologists were digging Anstead was able to cause mayhem. Anstead placed Inuit remains, fish bones from the Mediterranean, and tusks from the Sabre-Toothed tiger. There was so much confusion when these things were found that the Peruvian government established a whole Institute to try to explain it. Around the archaeology of these artefacts had grown an entire institute of study. A few bits and pieces from all over the world dumped in one place had the experts talking about trade routes and initiation ceremonies and the like.

Now whilst one would have perhaps expected Anstead to have felt guilty about all this, he didn't. In fact, it was one of his greatest achievements. He guffawed and chortled and beamed whenever he had an opportunity to show off about his Peruvian achievement. Anstead liked his achievement because it showed that before you know it, facts and errors are mixed up together and are called truth. There were as many strange and spurious institutes and facts that Anstead had nothing to do with than those, he had intervened in.

Anstead, however, was alarmed. Like all employees he worried what would happen to him if his services were no longer needed. As he got older, he wondered about his retirement. Moreover, as he journeyed into the future more and more, he realised that more and more of his work was being done for him. Misinformation and disinformation were blooming. No longer was it necessary to make stories up because everyone was doing that anyway. Archaeologists were piecing the world together more and more badly themselves without Anstead's help. This wasn't so much because they couldn't put the parts together, but because the meaning of those parts was so very far away. Whilst it may have been possible to find and identify some artefacts, often it was impossible to grasp their meaning.

As Anstead watched this process, he began to learn that history was a process of web building. Things that got caught in the web were uncovered, accepted, and used, those things which were too heavy fell through. Nevertheless, the web grew, and it contained in it whatever it came across, one way or another.

6 Florian, for want of a better name

This story is about seizing the day (carpe diem) and evaluating danger. It also explores the tragedy of life cut short.

Caterpillars cannot tell you the day of the week even if they want to, because caterpillars have no mind for such things. A caterpillar's world is a world of leaves and of eating, neither days of the week nor hours of the day have any meaning for it, for every day is an eating day and every waking hour is a meal hour.

Florian was a caterpillar. Florian was of course not his real name because caterpillars have no need of names either. The idea of one caterpillar running into another and saying, 'Hi my name is Florian,' is just a bit ridiculous. Nevertheless, to tell a story the main character needs a name, and the name of this caterpillar, for the purposes of this story, is Florian.

In any case, Florian lived in a pot plant. It was an everyday sort of pot plant, and this pot plant lived in an everyday sort of bathroom. The pot plant grew in an everyday sort of way, as indeed did Florian.

However, Florian was actually a gifted sort of caterpillar because he had a big brain. Not big by human standards, not even big enough to think of the days of the week or even of having a name, but Florian had been given the gift of wondering.

It has long been said that 'curiosity killed the cat,' and it was possibly a good thing that Florian was both a caterpillar and knew nothing of sayings for Florian certainly had an over-developed sense of curiosity.

Florian, however, knew nothing of the amazing life of caterpillars and how their life cycle involved one of the most remarkable transformations known in the natural world. This did not interest Florian, for aside from the pot plant, he had developed an interest in the bathroom.

The pot plant was in a safe place on the shelf, and it received regular watering and plenty of light. Florian could eat *al fresco* on the sunny side of the pot near the window or he could climb inside to the juicier leaves deep in the undergrowth. If he felt adventurous, he could climb to the top of the plant and, if he wanted to laze around, he could nibble at the bottom of the plant.

But Florian thought that there must be more to life than eating the pot plant. In the first instance, he knew he would never eat the whole plant because as fast as he ate it, the leaves grew back. This might itself have been interesting enough to consider - but Florian, in addition to being a thinker, was an explorer. Every day he gazed out to the great sink of the north wall, the flushing chasm of the east, the showering falls of the west, and the deep oceanic depths of the south.

One Wednesday, though Florian of course did not know it was a Wednesday, for caterpillars have no need to know the days of the week, he took flight. Florian had had enough, he was going 'over the top.' Goodbye to the juicy leaves, goodbye to the dark inner recesses of the plant - it was the bathroom he was going to see, the four wonders of the bathroom world.

He clambered down the side of the pot, and down onto the shelf. He felt wild and free and threw his head back in anticipation and excitement. His bristles ruffled in the breeze. Never had Florian squirmed so fast. He was off, first, to see the great showery plunge which had long fascinated him. During the days he would sit in his pot plant munching away watching the water fall seemingly forever into the sublime swirling flood pools below. Where did the water go? Florian was determined to find out. He was a wild caterpillar now - there was nothing stopping him, and he sped towards the shower having never known anything before but the safe world of his pot plant.

Beside the shower was a towering glass wall sprinkled with water. Florian ascended it to get a better view. As water vapour fell all around him, he felt like he had never felt before. This was living, free from the pot plant he could just see from the corner of his eye. The energy of the water fathoming down from the sky was so unlike anything that he had known. He could feel the spray on his back and could breathe in the mist.

Yet as he stood there on the wall, he was unaware of the human body entering the shower. Florian was certain enough of his safety for he had never been troubled by humans though he had seen them often enough. In fact, he felt proud that he and a human should both be witnessing this fountain together, creation admiring creation jointly.

As the huge human form moved into the shower, a deluge of water splashed onto the wall of the shower. Florian found himself slipping. He raced against the flow, but still he slipped. He walked as fast as his sixteen little legs could carry him, but as he walked away from the flow, so it engulfed him, and he found himself sliding down the great glass wall. The swirling pools below him made sloshing and slurping noises and the floor of the bathroom quickly rose up to meet him. He flopped onto the tiles and was caught in a monstrous whirlpool. With every ounce of his strength, he tried to hold on, but it was no use. He was thrown into an inescapable torrent as he gasped, and his sixteen feet grabbed for all their might. The drain was now so near he could see it glinting in the morning light. But this was the last light he was to see. The metal holes consumed him.

Florian was gone.

7 Renata

This is a story about a girl who realises in her dreams that, as far as she knows, there is no reason to believe that she actually existed at all. Reflecting on this idea she finds a way to believe in her own existence. This story challenges even the most basic things that are taken for granted in life.

Renata, like most of the characters in this book, was a bit of a thinker and perhaps also like some of the characters in this book, she was also something of a dreamer. She lived in a city in France in Brittany where her father sat on the local council called the *conseil municipal*. They lived in a fine house with servants, and she had a good education in a good Roman Catholic school.

I have already said that Renata was a dreamer, but she was a dreamer not in the sense that she had great daydreams or even dreams of wealth and fame, for she had already tasted this, but she had great visions and imaginings throughout the night. Sometimes she would dream about circuses and then she would dream of tigers, and then she would dream of fires. Her night time imagination knew no bounds.

Her father and her mother were, from time to time, worried about her, especially when she would shriek from her bedroom. However, because she always seemed so balanced and sensible the next morning and day, they saw no reason to pursue the matter with the doctor.

All her dreams were wild, colourful, tumultuous events set in grand locations, each, seemingly, with casts of thousands. Every moment was larger than life and filled with excitement and intrigue. Renata loved her dreams; they were her reason for living. Daytime was boredom; moments of waking that inconsiderately separated her from her dream world.

Sometimes she would tell her dreams to her mother who at first was interested and then became increasingly fearful of them. She tried telling the maid, but on one occasion she ran away screaming; for Renata had the ability to tell the stories of her dreams with almost as much realism and terror as she encountered them.

One day in July, during the summer heat, Renata had a new kind of dream. It was like no other dream that she had had before. As she lay in her bed glowing in the warmth, she was, in her dream, transported into an enormous space. There she spun around and around, like a wheel in a chasm of darkness and silence. On the first night, she spun around and around for hours.

Renata woke the next morning somewhat exhausted. This dream was far less sensible than the normal sorts of stories her mind would conjure for her. She had no idea what her dream meant. She desperately wanted the day to collapse so she could re-enter the mysterious night world to continue the scene, but sadly, she had to go to school.

As ever, school dragged on and on, and as much as Renata was getting the best education she could, she was often bored stiff. She did well at school, but regarded almost all of her peers as somewhat dim and even some of the teachers were a little on the slow side. The time after school, too, dragged on and on and on. Supper dragged on and on and on. Prayers dragged on and on and on. Then finally came sleep. Renata was excited, for this dream was a real mystery and she knew she would find out more this very night. Yet, as she lay there in restless expectation, she could of course not sleep, because she was spending time trying to understand what it was that this dream could have meant.

Eventually, sleep fell upon her. That night she was again transported into a swirling world, but this time there was less swimming in her vision. In this dark void she noticed that she was beginning to disappear. This was not a dream she thought, but a nightmare - she woke with a start.

She went out into the hallway to look out at the clock in the square. It was two in the morning. She went back to bed to think about her dream. She was beginning to disappear and perhaps before long she would disappear altogether. Not only that, but she had a premonition that this peculiar dream would come true and that unless she unlocked the key to this dream, she would soon be gone.

She stayed up from two in the morning until the time she had to go to school, thinking about the dream. How could it be that she was to disappear? How could she rescue herself? What could be stealing from her the power to exist? She wondered how it was that all the truths she knew of herself, could disappear. She wondered what she could do to fight from vanishing.

She decided that the enemy of truth had to be falsehood, and therefore to stop her disappearance, to offset the end of her truths, she would have to banish falsehood.

"How can a twelve-year-old girl banish falsehood?" she asked herself, "That's a rather metaphysical expectation for a young girl."

That day she went to school troubled, and her mother and her father, who could see something was wrong exchanged worried glances other over the breakfast table.

"Are you well my dear?" asked her father.

"Quite well," replied Renata.

 "I am pleased," he said.

Of course, Renata was *not* quite well, but her father's reply sat uneasily with her. *How* did my father content himself that I was well, she thought, because I had told him only of what I thought of my well-being. At the breakfast table, as she scooped out her egg, she thought to herself that it was *thinking* that dispelled falsehood; it was *reason*. She may not have been quite well, and her father may have been misled, but still, reason was the weapon for dispelling untruth.

That night after another tiresome day at school, Renata was again thrown into her dream world. She noticed that her body was beginning to wither away and disappear altogether. But this time she did not wake with a start, but instead woke gradually and did more thinking in that kind of halfway zone between waking and sleeping. In this state she thought that she would have to prove to herself that she existed in order to reclaim herself in her mind.
How could she prove that she was real - how did she know she was real? She was real because she *knew* it. Renata did not want to be misled as her father had been that morning, so her reasoning had to be certain. There was no room for error.

Renata knew lots of things that were not real (such as elves, fairies, and leprechauns) and maybe, therefore, she was just like one of those things. That would not do. Then she thought she must be real because she could see herself. She felt better for a moment, until she realised that she could see optical illusions, and that would not be real, perhaps she was an optical illusion. Then she thought that she must be real because *she thought* - not that she thought she was real, but just that she thought. If I can think, she thought, I must exist. If I can hold a thought, I must exist, I simply have to exist. A thing cannot hold a thought if it does not exist.

Just at that moment she drifted back off into sleep back into the darkness from where she had come. She again saw the big black nothingness, but she saw her fingers and her toes slowly reappear. However, as she watched her limbs reappear, she noticed out of the corner of her eye, that the world around her, which had by this time come into focus, was itself now beginning to disappear in the same way.

In the morning she felt good. She felt as if she had achieved something, as if she had unlocked an important key in understanding how things were true and how to banish falsehood. But how could she be sure that everything else around her existed – she still had to rescue everything else.

8 The World Department Store

This is a story about the developing world and how we are protected from knowing what it is like even though we are directly connected to it.

For weeks, it seemed, I walked past a building site, watching as the builders erected walls, glaziers installed windows, and pavers built pathways and a car park. The sign at the edge of the site read, "World Department Store - Factory Outlet. Bargains from around the world. Unbelievable value."

Being inquisitive, and a bit of a keen shopper, I was very interested. My mother always said to me, "Cosmo, I'm glad you're inquisitive." But despite this, as I am sure you are aware, parents are never over generous with the *moolah.** They were always out there buying new cars, golf clubs, dresses and shoes, when all you wanted was a simple new game for the PlayStation. It always seems to take months of careful pleading, negotiating, and reminding to get anywhere. The World Department Store looked like a good opportunity for a little *moolah* to go a long way, as I had to make do with what I had saved of my own modest pocket money income if I were to be able to buy anything.

In any case, this department store had me intrigued. It seemed that even if it were a rip-off, it would at least be worth a look. As the weeks passed, the place gradually began to take shape. Windows were polished, carpets were being fitted, and lighting was being installed. Then they started to put up signs showing what they had for sale, I guess to give a taster of what the bargains would be like.

What was on offer was fabulous, new stuff and amazing prices. Brand new Adidas Cross Trainer, gel support shoes, 45p. Puma brand footballs in genuine leather, 30p. Reebok sportswear from 45p to 90p. Leather jackets for £2.95. There was also genuine teak garden furniture - £2.70 for a beautiful chair. There were even the most amazing rugs for £3.00. It seemed so incredible. This was one place I was going to head for when it opened its doors. I looked carefully at the sign for information about the opening day. After reading all the advertising, at the bottom of the sign it said, "The World Department Store - Factory Outlet opens on 8th October - shop early for Christmas." Now this was only a week away; I would be there at 3.30pm sharp, straight after school. I couldn't wait.

In the days leading up to the 8th, I counted my pocket money over and over. I emptied out my moneybox, I did errands for Dad, and I even recalled in the loans I made to my brother. Altogether I had £8.08. Not as much usual, but it should be a king's ransom at The World Department Store - Factory Outlet.

School on Wednesday dragged on, but finally the bell rang, and I was out of the gate like lightning.

When I got to the shop, there was a great red carpet on which customers entered the store. I guessed that was what was meant by the 'red carpet treatment.'

"Wow, this is great," I thought as I walked in passed the doorman who opened the door for me.
"Good afternoon, Sir," said the doorman.

"I could get used to this," I thought.

"Good afternoon, doorman," I replied pompously.

"Isn't this posh?" I thought to myself.

However, just then, a funny thing happened. As I entered the shop, I encountered something I just didn't expect. It smelt. The store smelt. Not like a city department store might with wafts of expensive perfume and freshly baked bread from the food hall. It smelt like sweat - stinky body odour. It was the rancid smell of sweaty bodies.

Inside the cavernous department store the main hall was set up with tables filled with interesting things to buy. I rushed through the store to see whether the bargains, which had been advertised on the sign outside, were really there or whether it was all some sort of hoax. Although, quite frankly, I had been doubtful that all the advertised items would be there, I was surprised to find, they were all there and there were many genuine named brands being sold for next to nothing. Amazing bargains were everywhere. I rushed around the whole store deciding what to buy, and there was so much to see. I bought a football, and some shoes and some cool football ornaments for my bedroom. I had bought all these things and I still had more than 4 pounds left. I was so excited that I sat on a bench and decided to look at my purchases before I bought more.

I sat just outside the Adidas section of the store, and it was there that I noticed the smell again - but there was more than just a smell that made this place odd. It was hot, in fact much much hotter than your usual air-conditioned department store would be. In fact, I guess it must have been about thirty-five degrees in there, and it was humid too. The perspiration was pouring off my face.

Then something even more odd happened. As I sat there, I felt a tugging at my shirt. I nearly jumped out of my skin because there was a hand grabbing at my shirt through a hole in the wall. But it wasn't the hand of an adult; it was the hand of a child. I jumped up and pushed the hand away and was ready to run off when I decided to have a look through this curious gap in the wall.

I peered in and through the wall I could see scores of children working at machinery and lifting heavy boxes. It also became quite clear, looking through the gap, where the smell was coming from.

"Help us, look, this is how we have to live - if we try to escape, we are beaten," said a pleading voice through the wall.

This was a pretty scary experience for me, and it was certainly one that I was not expecting to have in a department store in the 21st century. I leapt up and ran away from the bench by the wall. I didn't know what to think … what *was* this place anyway?

Soon I was enticed by yet more bargains, a rug the size of a sofa for £4.00. It would look great in my room. You couldn't go wrong for four quid even if you got sick of it.

"Sir, can I interest you in a lovely dhurrie rug? The cost to you today, Sir, £4.00," asked the man obsequiously. Just as I was thinking about making a purchase, I saw again through the wall behind the stall, a battery of children at looms. I could hear the machinery whirring and the smell was just as strong here. This whole set-up was strange, and I was beginning to feel very uncomfortable. It was time to leave this place and I wasn't sure, despite the bargains, whether I would want to come back. I took my football, and my boots and followed the red carpet back out of the store.

As the porter opened the door and gave me a broad, if rather creepy smile, I realised again how much I had been sweating. I felt round the back of my neck and realised that the pillow on which I had been lying was drenched with perspiration. I woke with a start. It was one of those vivid dreams that seemed so very real. The funny thing was that I realised that the items I had bought in The World Department Store were items that I already owned. It was true but just how could this be?

There in the corner of my bedroom was a pair of Adidas Cross Trainer gel support trainers and a Puma football. My parents had bought these things for me during the year.

Why were those things in my dream? What was so special about those two things? Where *did* those things come from before my parents bought them?

*moolah – is an old word meaning money.

9 Ermonza

This story is about conscience and the way that people around us, through the way we live with them, contribute to who we are and what we believe. It looks at recognising individual heritage, valuing those around us and using their commitment to us to our best advantage.

Ermonza clenched her fists, her shoulders tensed, and her face contorted. It was happening again. She spun round, furious, making sure not to look anyone in the face, stomped up the hallway, slammed the front door open and went to her bike. She made sure that she knocked over the pot plant on the veranda as she spun her means of escape around, hitting the back wheel against the wall of the house, which, as the house was made of wood, made a great thud. She pedalled hard up the driveway and away.

Everyone in the house looked agog at each other. It wasn't that Ermonza didn't always go off in a huff when she didn't get her own way, but today's performance was, perhaps, a little over-acted. No one of course would ever tell her so because that might be dangerous. After a moment everyone politely smiled at each other and went back about their business. Ermonza, however, still had steam piping out of her ears.

A bike ride, was, however, just the thing that Ermonza needed, she needed the fresh air, the freedom, and the opportunity to sprint off into another world and then meander as one can only really do on a bike.

Secretly Ermonza also knew that she had over-reacted, but a bike ride was better when it was had a purpose. To Ermonza, riding her bike was like chopping wood, it was a chance to take out aggression on the road, or the pedals or the bike or all of the above if necessary. And then, as the mood changed, the bike would be a means to another end, it afforded silent, smooth coasting along the road, or grassy verges or anywhere really. But it wasn't really the wandering of the bike that was so valuable to Ermonza, but it was the wandering of the mind that one could do whilst wandering on the bike. It was as if the very to and fro-ing of the bike was just the right thing to be doing when your mind was to and fro-ing as well.

Ermonza rode to the river, which was a fair old trip, on a bike at least. But riding hard made her relax; the cool breeze in her face, and the ever-changing array of things to notice, or to just cycle past.

Ermonza liked to think. She liked to get worked up about people, and she liked to imagine things that might happen to them. Sometimes when she was in a good mood, she might imagine good things and at other times she might imagine things so horrid that they ought not be spelt out here. Sometimes when she found her thoughts wandering into these places, she could imagine someone else saying, 'How could you say that? I would never wish that on anyone.' But, on her journeys, her bike was her only companion, and it never said a thing.

She was deliciously alone. In a world of her thoughts no one could disturb her there. She could go anywhere, even beyond the bounds of believability. Should some horrid misadventure befall her, so long as her brain functioned, she would be all right. She could forever play in the forest of her mind. Here she was never bored, or vexed, or chased, unless of course she wanted to be.

Ermonza got off her bike and sat on the tree stump at her favourite place along the river. Here she could see the current and the water running over the tree roots. Looking down along the river she could see a much wider, shallower patch. Here one could wade, one could swim, and on the other, deeper side of the river, one could even dive. There was fruit too. Many years ago, orange trees were planted in a small orchard. If ever there was a Garden of Eden, then this was it, at least for Ermonza. It wasn't even possible to do the wrong thing here because there were no apples or serpents, just oranges.

Ermonza lay back against the other part of the tree, the part that had not been cut off and resumed the position of comfortable thinking where she could truly leave the fiery cauldron of the place that she, reluctantly, called home.

This day she thought of JJ, and of his silly taunts. Wouldn't it be wonderful if every time JJ spoke, he put his foot in his mouth and said something really stupid. Ermonza pictured her mother's kitchen and played out various arguments as they had happened in the past and JJ constantly fumbling for words, instead of being the articulate, confident boy that he was.

But today Ermonza's fanciful imaginings were to be invaded. Invaded by just a little too much reality. For some reason, and she couldn't fathom why, she found the people who, in her dreamy imagination, she would often make behave in the most ridiculous of ways, would just not do as they were told. It was as if her conscience had swelled up and refused to accept too much deviation from the truth. This was not to Ermonza's liking! When Ermonza turned JJ into a frog,

JJ would amazingly morph back into an arrogant and annoying brother. When she had her mother velcroed to the kitchen ceiling, she would nonchalantly, unfasten herself and float back down to the floor. When her father was glued to the toilet seat, he would miraculously detach himself and then wander back into the living room.

Ermonza, had no idea what to do. It was like a waking nightmare. How could one's imaginings be so infected? What the Dickens was going on?

Ermonza cried. She sat at the edge of the river, looking at the place that she loved so much, and she cried. She cried because her own imaginings had been infiltrated by the very people she was getting away from. All of a sudden, she felt very alone. There, in her head, were all the people she was trying to avoid, and she felt so horribly alone.

She tried again, to re-enter her imaginings, but her parents and her brother were intractable. There was a little too much truth for Ermonza to deal with.

"Where to now?" she thought, given that her only retreat, her previously impregnable imagination world, was broken. "How can this be true?" she thought. "Where is there for me to go, which path should I take, and should the path I take be on the road with my bike, or in my head?"

What a predicament she was in and how miserable all this was making her. She sat there and continued to cry and then, in her emptiness, JJ approached her, and her mother and father, but they were far from sympathetic.

"Stop blubbing, you only have yourself to blame."
"Look at you, so filled up with your own self-interest, what about everyone else around you, have you bothered even to give them a thought?"
"Come on Sis, look at you, pull yourself together."

This was the last straw. Ermonza was ready to throw herself in the river to let the cold water wash all this confusion away when she had an idea. She decided to imagine visiting Aunt Francesca. Aunt Francesca and she never argued, her mother said that they were like 'peas in a pod.' Ermonza knew that owing to her years she had a tad more experience and wisdom than did one twelve-year-old girl. Ermonza knew Aunt Francesca would know what to do.

But Ermonza hesitated; in fact, she felt quite odd, and she shook. She feared thinking about Aunt Francesca in case she too had been drawn into this newly perplexing and frightening world of her mind. She wondered whether bringing Aunt Francesca into her thoughts would change her forever. Someone who had been always an ally may become an adversary like the rest of her family.

She imagined Aunt Francesca, entering her living room in a business-like and carefree way. What would she say? How would she react? Would she support the taunts of the others or be drawn to Ermonza and the way she had seen things.

"My dear," explained Aunt Francesca, "when all else fails, try conciliation. Try being agreeable."

"Conciliation," thought Ermonza, "that's something that I hadn't properly thought of," she ruminated. "It's a bit drastic, but it just might work."

"Remember dearest Ermonza," called Aunt Francesca, "you're never really alone, your entire family as well as me, we're all in your head at the same time, and you're there too. Listen, listen, and think about the others who are with you, they will always be there, and it's better if they're friendly. It may well be that sometimes others are wrong, but you need to listen and always, always to think. If conciliation is needed, you will know it, and it will be clearly the right thing, even if it may be the hardest. Everyone who has had anything to do with you, even in the smallest way, is there inside your head too. They make up who you are. Take the best things from each of them and build them into yourself. The solutions to your problems come from within. Don't lament that all these people are with you; get their help, use them as resources.

Think, reflect, consider, and understand, and you will know what to do. Take care my love."

10 Mrs McCulvert lived alone

This story is about having a sense of purpose, about the resolution of loneliness and about kindness. The story also includes a theme of dying and of a peaceful end.

Mrs McCulvert lived alone in a small house in the suburban area called Savannah Hills. Savanah Hills became very hot during the summer and Mrs McCulvert was never good with the heat. She didn't even know why she lived there. It was just where she ended up. Mrs McCulvert didn't like to think about it, but it was clear that she was never going to move house. This house would 'see her out.' She looked around the room and thought, 'I wonder whether it will be in the armchair over there, or in the garden. Perhaps I shall be in bed. Perhaps I shall fall off a ladder. Perhaps… oh, how ridiculous that I should be thinking like this,' she thought to herself, and she went into the kitchen, took the tea from the cupboard, and put the kettle on.

Mrs McCulvert had very few visitors, and when she did have them, she was always suspicious. She lived alone, never really seeing anyone, or speaking to many people at all. Sometimes salespeople telephoned her trying to sell her roof guttering, or vacuum cleaners or things like that. She enjoyed speaking to them, but of course she didn't know who they were, and they didn't know who she was, and she knew they really didn't care 'two hoots' about her. But that was OK, because she didn't care about them either, but still, it was nice to have a bit of a yarn. She never ever bought anything, but it was good to have a chat every now and then, even if it was just to know she was still capable of conversation.

The only other person who Mrs McCulvert spoke to was William. William Russell lived next door and, from time to time, his ball would come over the fence, and he would knock on the door and ask whether he could go round the back and get his ball.

She always said, "Well William, your ball again, well, go round and get it then, that's a good boy."

Then she would sit back down in her armchair and continue watching the telly or doing the crossword or knitting or whatever she was doing at the time.

Mrs McCulvert got to thinking again about her last days, whenever they might be. She thought, it would be nice to have someone to talk to about all the things in her house and what they meant to her, and to tell them about where she grew up and about her mother, and her father, and about her life. Otherwise, she thought that it would all just float away when she was gone. But the only one she could ask would be William. But what would an eleven-year-old boy want to know about the contents of an old lady's soul? She sat in her armchair deflated. She looked around at the walls of her living room, everyone covered with shelves of trinkets. Little collected things from days gone by. There they sat, year in, year out, as steadfast as a ship in mud. She wondered whether the books and the figurines and the bits and bobs, would ever take root. She wondered what her house would be like in a thousand years if no one touched it.

She looked out of her window and there was William playing with his basketball. How she hated the noise of the ball hitting the concrete. Thankfully, he only seemed to ever play for about half an hour. Mrs McCulvert made a cup of tea and sat in the kitchen looking over the back fence. She wondered whether William would be a willing confidant.* She looked at him through the window, and she asked herself the question, 'Would I, as a young girl, have been interested in the muddled thoughts of an old woman?'

She thought for a moment, 'No' she thought, but then she remembered her brother, the brother who she had loved so dearly and who had died of leukaemia as a small boy. When he was in hospital, he spent endless hours talking to the old lady who was in the bed beside him at the hospital. So maybe it would be possible, she thought. It would all depend on the boy, she guessed.

Week after week she would look out at William playing basketball. She must have consumed a lot of tea during this time. She found herself hoping that the ball would come over the fence. She watched as it bounced and virtually pleaded with the ball to get over the fence so that William would have to come to the door. Weeks and weeks went by and William, perhaps because of the heat or perhaps through boredom seemed to play less and less basketball and Mrs McCulvert felt that she had found, like all her collecting, yet another lost cause and that William had lost interest in her, if fact he was ever interested at all.

She took to taking her tea in the living room again, far from the window which looked over the Russell's yard. She now seldom heard William's basketball and presumed that he had found some new indoor pursuit or something more agreeable to do. At least there was peace and quiet again. She sat back on her sofa and looked up at the small flowery teapot that was on display on the top shelf of the China cabinet. It was only a cheap thing, but her mother had bought it for her on the day of her twenty-first birthday, almost seventy years ago. She remembered the tea parties she would have and the times she served tea from it.

Even without using it she remembered that it poured particularly well, she could remember its weight, and the chink sound of the lid. She knew that the handle had a little chip out of it. All this she knew, and the teapot had been sitting on that shelf unused now for almost twenty-five years.

She looked around again at all the things on the shelves and a tear came to her eye. What a sad and lonely life she had led, and all as a little girl who was known for her liveliness and her interest in people and places. She wiped her eye and told herself not to be 'so soft.'

As she sat dabbing her eyes, there was an almighty crash. A sound so loud that it made Mrs McCulvert's heart skip a beat. She got up and looked into the kitchen and the tea cupboard had collapsed onto the floor and all the China had been smashed. It had made quite an awful noise.

William appeared at the door and peered in through the fly screen window. "Mrs McCulvert, Mrs McCulvert, are you alright? Mrs McCulvert."

"William, William, come in, I'm just a bit shocked that's all, the tea cupboard collapsed and all the China's smashed."

William let himself in to see that she was alright, and he caught a glimpse of the mess of wood and China littered all over the floor of the kitchen.

"Look at the mess, Mrs McCulvert," said William shocked to see such a pile of rubble.

"Don't worry my boy," she replied, "I'll clean it up. Look at all my lovely plates and things, all broken."

"Don't worry Mrs McCulvert, I'll help you. You just sit down here and tell me what to do and I'll do it for you. Would you like me to make you a cup of tea?"

"My dear boy, all the tea things are destroyed!"

"Don't worry Mrs McCulvert, I'll be right back."

Mrs McCulvert caught her breath as William dashed out of the door. Although she was shocked, she began to realise what a propitious act the collapse of the shelf had been. 'All that china smashed to bits,' she thought. 'What the hell, they're only plates,' she thought as she smiled, feeling better already.

William reappeared with a piping hot mug of tea. "I was going to bring you cup and saucer, but you get more tea in a mug," he said.

"Thank you, my boy," she replied.

"Mum said I should help you clean up. She was going to come herself, but I told her that I had it all under control. But she'll come if you like."

"I'm sure we can manage it."

Mrs McCulvert sat in the large armchair and looked into the kitchen as William carried out the bits of wood from the shelves and stacked them outside. As the shelf had fallen it had broken apart, and it all was well beyond repair.

"Oh William," she called out as he grabbed the bits of china that needed to be flung into the bin. "William, on that plate there once stood a great blancmange† which one a very important cooking competition in 1956. Off that plate I served blancmange to the whole tennis club, every Tuesday afternoon for more than a year…and now look at it."

"It's a waste, Mrs McCulvert, but it's only a plate."

"Right you are William, right you are, it is only a plate, and look at me, I am surrounded by plates, and saucers, and tea pots. Perhaps I have become a plate in my old age!" she grinned.

"Perhaps, Mrs McCulvert, perhaps you have! Mrs McCulvert, the old plate, me mate," replied William smiling too.

It wasn't long after that that Mrs McCulvert died peacefully in her sleep. She was found by the milkman who had noticed that she hadn't collected the milk in. William and his family went to the funeral. They were the only ones there.

Within a week a large van had come to collect all her belongings. Her knick-knacks, and her dresses, her socks, and her rolls of sticky tape, and her old newspapers and her toenail clippers, and her cushions and her jars of this and that, and her earrings and her seats and bedding and curtains and other bits and bobs. All these things went into the truck. And when the truck left the house was quite empty.

William asked his mother what would happen to all Mrs McCulvert's things, and she said that they would all go off to auction. William felt sad that so many of Mrs McCulvert's things, which had so much value to her would probably be sold as junk. People would come by and pick up some old thing that Mrs McCulvert had treasured all her life, and take one look at it and say, 'Who'd ever buy that ugly thing.' Others would come and look at collection of Mrs McCulvert's entire life and say, 'What a lot of old junk.'

William felt sad at the thought of all this. What he didn't know was that after speaking to William just weeks before, she had decided that all her whole collection of bits and bobs was in fact not as important as she had once thought, and she saw it all just as flotsam and jetsam,** just as the mere accumulation of things. She felt strangely relieved as she died – not that William was ever to know.

* confidant – someone who you can tell something to, who isn't going to tell everyone else.

† blancmange – pronounced *bluh-monj* is a sweet creamy dessert.

** flotsam and jetsam – nautical terms that relate to shipwrecks and bits that are left in the sea after a ship has sunk or after items have been thrown off.

11 André and the Toaster

This story is about the design idea that an object should look like what it does. Not all things are like this, and many consider that if the shape of something resembles what it does, then the object is well designed, because you can tell what it does and how it works by just looking at it.

Although André liked English, he sometimes thought that his English teacher, Mr Hopkins, was a bit batty. Having seen the film, Dead Poet's Society where the teacher acted in a peculiar way, he thought that Mr Hopkins had been trying for an Oscar for his performances.

Once Mr Hopkins asked each boy in the class to pretend to be a musical instrument and to write about it. 'How absurd,' thought André. Today Mr Hopkins was to make another attempt at the Oscar for 'Silliest Teacher in the History of Education.' 'The nominations are…' he could hear the actress saying it as he gazed off into space. Mr Johnson for his impersonation of a fish, Mrs Boone for her clay model of inspiration, or Mr Hopkins and his analysis of a toaster.'

"André, my dear boy," said Mr Hopkins, "you are doing it again, you are gazing at the ceiling and smiling. What is it, may I ask, that you find so amusing about the ceiling in 5a? Is it the delicate play of light on the patterned ceiling, is it the spit balls that dot the ceiling's surface reminding you of some previously visited lunar landscape?"

There was a peal of laughter from the class. "I'm sorry Mr Hopkins," said André caught off guard. But, finding his feet again quickly and having to find face after having been admonished, he called out, "Sir, it just seems that spending a whole homework on writing about the toaster seems, well, very peculiar, and quite frankly a waste of time."

"The way that Shakespeare wrote was peculiar when he did it André, that's the whole point."

The bell rang, and Mr Hopkins said, "Before you go, remember, I want five hundred words about your toaster."

André got up from his seat, and as this was the last lesson of the day, proceeded to walk to the bus. The bus stop was next to an electrical appliance shop, just around the corner from the library. André looked in the window as he waited for the bus. In the window was an array of electrical things such as: juicers, electric knives, waffle irons, milkshake makers, coffee grinders, can openers, blenders, food processors, irons, kettles and toasters.

Having never thought much about toasters, he went into the shop where he said to the sales assistant, "I would like you to show me your toaster range." The sales assistant, a little surprised that a twelve-year-old boy would be interested in toasters, nevertheless, obliged.

"This, Sir, is our range of toasters," he said.

"Well," said André, "what's the difference between them?"

The sales assistant showed him the range telling him about the ones with the auto-lift mechanisms, the ones with both automatic and variable colour control, he told him about cool-wall toasters, and stainless-steel toasters, and toasters in the lifestyle range.

"The lifestyle range!" exclaimed André, "Who would ever base their lifestyle on a toaster?" asked André, who started to think about the Oscar awards for the 'Design of Silly Toasters.' "How ridiculous!" said André as he stormed out of the shop.

"Do I take it, Sir, that you are no longer interested in purchasing a toaster?"

"I never had any intention of buying a toaster," said André as he rushed past the quizzical sales assistant.

André boarded his bus and looked out of the window at the streetscape as he went home.

Despite his seeming disrespect for the humble toaster, André's secret pleasure was eating peanut butter and jam on toast as soon as he got home from school. As he got home, he slung his bag on the porch, and flung the door open.

"I'm home," he shouted as he came in the door. His mother came out of the living room and gave the boy a kiss. "Mother, I'm getting a little old for this everyday now."

"André, don't be ridiculous, sometimes you say the oddest things," said his mother. "Dear, I have a surprise for you, well just a little surprise – I bought a new toaster."

Now there's a coincidence you'd only find in a short story, thought André.

"It's a fabulous new toaster, and I put the peanut butter and jam by its side for you dear. It's part of the Lifestyle range."

"Good grief!" said André. "Well Mum, I guess you've got to get points for helping me with my homework?"

"Strange boy," said his mother.

André pulled a stool up and sat at the bench gazing into the shiny side of the General Electric, stainless steel, sensor-controlled, internal crumb tray, cool-wall, Lifestyle toaster.

"Does it have a remote control, Mum?" grinned André.

"Now you're being quite ridiculous," harrumphed his mother.

"Well, that's how I'm supposed to be, or so says Mr Hopkins."

"I wonder *what* they teach you in that school?"

André put two pieces of bread in the toaster and watched as the little motor drew the bread slowly down into the toasting chamber. "Cool, but a little unnecessary," he thought.

The toast that the Lifestyle toaster made was very good, as far as toast went. He said to his mother, as his stomach gradually filled, "Mum, Man cannot live on bread alone, but with toast, he can get pretty close."

André's mother had given up saying anything and she just shook her head. She had long grown used to her quite unusual son.

André went to get his notebook thinking that this was probably the best time to do his homework.

André looked at the toaster. He wondered what sort of lifestyle one was meant to have with a toaster like this. He wondered whether the lifestyle in his house was a suitable one. He wondered whether the toaster would be happy at 21b North Parade. He wondered what sort of toaster it might be and what it would rather have been doing. He thought of the toaster a bit like Buzz Lightyear, thinking himself quite a grand appliance when he was merely a toy.

How could one tell what sort of thing the toaster would like? The only clue was how it looked. It was all bright and shiny. It had a little orange light that showed that it was operating, and it was at the cutting edge in industrial design. It was quite out of place here André thought. André's kitchen was not at all like this, it was filled with older things, bits and pieces of all different ages. This toaster must be rather miserable here, he thought.

André wondered, other than make toast, what this toaster was designed to do. One thing that worried him about its design, was that it was very streamlined.

Streamlining, found on cars and planes and ships, had only one function that he knew, and that was to allow something to be propelled more efficiently. One made an object streamlined, if it needed to go through the air, like a plane, or a car, or something like that.

It suddenly dawned on André. He had worked it out, it was obvious. He had no idea why it had taken him so long to work it out. This toaster was designed to fly.

André found himself almost feeling sorry for the toaster, in that it had been brought into this kitchen which was obviously a much less grand kitchen than it had ever been designed to grace. It must have been crying its little circuits out. André knew what he had to do, even if it would be very difficult to explain to his mother.

André grabbed the toaster, unplugged it from the wall and flung it out of the window. André stood there with his hands on the sash looking down as the toaster flew down the two stories that there were to the ground. He watched as the toaster, with its cord hanging free, slipping through the air making use of its astonishingly low drag factor, gliding inexorably downwards towards its final moment. He smiled as it crashed, the moment of glory like a kamikaze, he thought.

He opened his notebook, "Death of a Toaster: A moment of glory," he wrote.

12 Inevitability

This story deals with inevitability and is the form of a 'choose your own story' format. If reading to a group, you might want to ask group members to vote on decisions that have to be made. The story is quite short, so not too many decisions are called for. Nevertheless, at the end the reader will want to read the alternatives not chosen. The reader is Boris. The first section introduces the situation Boris is in, and then the reader becomes Boris.

Boris woke with a start and found himself in a cave. The cave smelt of evil. Around him in the darkness he could just make out a small light. The light was so dim he could not tell how far away it was and having no other means to know where to go, or any other way to tell where he was, he headed for the light. He advanced slowly, feeling the ground below him, which were in parts rocky and in other parts strangely spongy.

He seemed to spend hours getting to the faint light. It could have been many hundreds of metres that had walked, or it could have been relatively few. He could not even properly tell how big the steps he was taking were because the ground was so uneven. When, finally, he came to the source of the light he could see that it came from a door. From the gaps in the door, the light trickled out as if from a fountain whose water pressure was too low. Not knowing what else to do, he opened it.

Behind the door was a great light, a light so bright that he had to close his eyes. Having been in almost total darkness for so long the brilliance gave him an immediate head-spin and it took him some time for his eyes to adjust. (Look up at the sky - though not the sun - and feel the light in your eyes. Imagine that you were Boris getting used to the light in this new, enormous space. Look up at the sky or a bright room lamp for at a few moments.) (Don't stare at a light that is too bright!)

When Boris's eyes adjusted, he could see before him some writing, writing that seemed to be floating in the space in front of him something like a holographic image. (Hold the book up, in front of your eyes).

For you have landed in this place
You know not which way you face
There are dangers here for you
Choose correctly or you will lose

Would you like a journey foreign?
To a place where up is down
Evil springs from a flowing well-spring

Font of darkness for a crown

Turn you right for a watery voyage
Turn you left for an airborne treat
Make a mistake and be discouraged
By the loss of hands and feet

Turn right: go to Option A1
Turn left: go to Option A2

[The reader becomes Boris.]

Option A1

Water is all around you. You don't know what to do. Again, it is dark. Big silent sea creatures swim around you and above you. You can see light and the passing of a boat. Up you swim, the air emptying from your lungs. You are sure you are going blue, but to get to the surface in time is your only hope. You are flailing your arms and legs and trying not to let water into your mouth. The boat gets larger oh so slowly. Your head is throbbing, and you feel yourself losing consciousness and yet you are wriggling and heading for the surface. You fight and kick and push and finally the air. The sweet, sweet air. You suck it in like it was your first breath and feel the air fill your lungs as your heart pumps as fast as it can to send the new oxygen into every corner of your body. You smell the air and feel glad to be alive. [Take three big deep breaths, no more, and smell the air.]

Then after a minute, whilst your body gets over the shock of near death, you notice in the air the smell of diesel, fuel and around you in the fog you can make out the shape of boats and hear their sounds. You realise that you are afloat amongst a flotilla of great ships, any one of which could collide with you at any moment. You start to notice now that you are cold and wet.

What do you do?

Option B1: Stay still to preserve your energy and scream out.
Option B2: Swim as far and as hard as possible in the direction that the ships are going.
Option B3: Swim as far and as hard as possible in the direction that the ships coming from.
Option B4: Dive and look for hope in the depths.

Option B1
You choose to stay and call out. Although the ships are big, you decided that there would always be people on deck, on watch. Your chances are good because you can tread water well and because there were so many ships, there must be many people watching, especially because of the fog.

You call out, "Help, help, SOS, SOS, save me, save me." But the ships carry on relentlessly. You wonder now whether this had been a good idea, and you call even more strongly. It seems that you have been in the water now for an hour. The coldness is seeping into your bones, and you can feel your legs starting to cramp and freeze up. You watch as the last ship cruises past.

Weakened by your struggle, you are consumed by the sea. Go to Option D5

Option B2
You choose to swim as far and as hard as possible in the direction that the ships are heading. They seem not to be going so fast, and their engines seemed to not be making that much noise. They must be slowing down. At one point you even think you see a tugboat in the fog, a sure sign that their destination was near. You swim and occasionally you stop to see the boats, but they are still there. After catching your breath, you realise that swimming *was* the best option because you are a strong swimmer.

From time to time as you stop to check the position of the ships, you start to notice that the fog is lifting, and you think you can even see land ahead. You swim now with all your energy hoping to see the land and maybe to catch the attention of those on the shore. But when you lift your head after swimming continuously for about half an hour, you realise that you had been wrong.

The fog has lifted, and you can now see all the way out to sea with no sign of land. The ships too are leaving you and their lights sail off into the distance despite your shouting and waving.

Exhausted and disheartened, you are consumed by the sea. Go to Option D5.

Option B3

You choose to swim as fast and as hard as possible in the direction the ships are coming from. It seems that it is quite likely that they have just left because, although their engines are making a lot of noise, they don't seem to be going at full speed. This, you think, is surely the sign that they have just left and are trying to pick up speed and must still be near the shore. You swim as hard and as fast as you can. As you swim you can see the fog lifting just a little. In fact, you can see lights by the shore. You were right, the shore is just a couple of hundred metres away. You can see lights and people and you can even hear music. Surely you have made the right choice. You swim for the shore as fast as you can. As you get closer you can feel the water of the sea getting warmer as you get closer, the water from the beach that you think had been heated by the sun by day, or perhaps it was the outwash from some pretty lagoon.

But as you swim, you feel your legs cramping up and you gradually become paralysed. One last ship fearful of being lost at the end of the fleet, sails close to you and you are caught up in the swirl of water. You are dragged beneath and are consumed by the sea. Go to D5.

Option B4
You choose to dive and look for an escape there. When you had been in the murky depths you seem to have recalled seeing some activity. Perhaps there would be a submarine to attract or perhaps there would be divers who would give you oxygen and collect you. It seemed a long shot, but there was no use staying afloat as no one would hear you. There was no use swimming because in your weakened state you would make little headway. Maybe your only chance was to seek activity beneath the sea.

You take a deep breath and do a duck dive to get below the water. Here are the murky depths you saw earlier. Here you could see again the groper fish and the little schools. If only you were a fish, you thought.

Then in the distance you saw them. Divers with lights and a sort of open submarine. They were loading trinkets from the sea. You swam towards them but then had to surface for more air. As before, you arose at the surface gasping and breathing in the sweetness of oxygen. But you were determined to find them, your only ray of hope. Down you dive again, but this time there is no finding the people you had just seen. Up you come for more air, and down again, time and time again.

You are feeling weak. There is little energy left in your body the cold water and the diving quickly saps anything you had left. Down you go again for the last time. Your energy gone, your legs frozen and cramping from the cold - you are consumed by the sea. Go to Option D5.

Option A2

Turning left, you realised that you had made a mistake because you could feel the floor dropping from beneath you, you looked down and below you were thousands of metres of land rising up from you at lightning speed. You were falling, as if from an aeroplane, but you did not know how you had come to be there. You grabbed around yourself to see if by some miracle you had been granted a parachute but no such luck. In fact, you were just as you had been in the cave, defenceless, and heading towards the earth at a frightening pace. Then around you, you could see other things falling from the sky with you. These must offer some hope because you alone had no chance of saving yourself.

Descending around you were countless objects as if they had been thrown out of a warehouse at ten thousand metres. You looked down and wondered how much time you had left. The planet seemed to be rising up faster than you liked.

In desperation you look around you. There is a large weather balloon and an inflator; there is a box marked military equipment (parachutes). There is also an enormous kite. There is a folded-up hang glider. All the things seemed to have been cooked up by fate to give some hope, but not one of them enough hope as to be the obvious choice. The earth was even closer.

How could I be expected to inflate a balloon whilst falling at this pace? Still, it might work. The parachutes seemed like a good idea, but I had never used a parachute before, nor did the wooden crates seem easily opened. The kite looked easier to get going, but you had never had a good experience flying a kite and certainly not whilst falling out of a plane! The hang glider might have been a sensible option but how do you open a hang glider at 200km/h.

Time was clearly running out. What did you choose?
Option C1: The Balloon
Option C2: The Parachutes
Option C3: The Enormous Kite
Option C4: The Hang Glider

Option C1
You chose the balloon. The balloon would gradually

reduce the lift and its air friction would slow you down you thought. If you landed in water, it would keep you afloat. You could see that the balloon was some sort of weather balloon that was very strong and designed to carry heavy duty weather equipment or even spy camera equipment, so it should hold the weight of a person. You flap your arms over to it and pull the lever labelled self-inflate. The balloon inflates to its maximum level and the gas canister shuts off.

As this seems to have happened in slow motion you could feel yourself gradually slowing down. You seem to be a little too heavy for the balloon, which is a good thing because it means that the balloon will want to go down rather than up. Your arms are becoming sore because of the pressure you must exert to hold on, but you know you can cope. You were amazed that your decision seemed to be working.

You thought to yourself that this must all be a trick. But as you descend you find that the balloon seems to be getting smaller and that you seem to be picking up speed. You realise that because of the change in air pressure the balloon is losing pressure, but the lever to the gas canister is jammed. There is now not enough upward pull to slow you down and you accelerate to the ground.

You meet the ground with mortal force. Go to Option D5.

Option C2
The Parachutes. You will fall out of the plane and head towards the ground at a pace. The parachute is naturally the only answer. You wave your arms about and get to the box. It is nailed shut. You push and shove and kick and scream and yank at the box, but it does not give. You hit the ground with mortal force. Go to Option D5.

Option C3
You choose the enormous kite. The parachute looks sealed up, the glider seems too difficult in such a short period of time and the balloon as useful as a brick - but maybe the kite could help. If you were to let it catch the wind and then climb the rope, you could let it draw you down carefully. You may get hurt, and it may not be pretty, but there is, or so you think, more hope in the kite than the other options.

The kite is not an everyday kite but an enormous kite, the kind they sometimes fly at kite shows, it was more like a parachute you thought. Folding it out quickly you pushed it aside to catch the wind. Catch the wind it did. You let a lot of rope out and tie the far end to your middle. Wrapping some of the rope round your arms you pull the rope in tight to pull up the slack to reduce the jolt you would get when you caught up with the rope.

And boy was there a jolt, but luckily for you the jolt is not too strong, and you find yourself swaying from the bottom of an enormous kite.

You are lucky, this seems to have been the right option. You were carried off away from the falling debris and towards the sea. A soft landing you thought, and someone would be sure to see you, you thought. You praised your good choice and even almost enjoyed the view.

The kite drew you off into the sea just as you thought, but on your landing, you became tangled in the rope and the kite itself. Unable to free yourself and tired by the struggle you are consumed by the sea. Go to Option D5.

Option C4

You choose the hang glider. Now whilst hang gliding wasn't exactly your thing you thought that the other options were least likely to save you. The balloon is not strong enough to hold a person, even if you could get it inflated. The parachute is fine if you could get the box open, and it looked quite securely fastened. The kite seems a ridiculous idea, but just perhaps there is hope with the hang glider.

A hang glider should fold out easily especially using the descending wind as leverage. If you could only get the thing open and gradually catch it in the wind by slowly tipping it up, there may be a chance. If you got it right, it would be like a flight to the land. None of the options seemed very hopeful and this, you think, is the best one (or the least bad one).

You fly yourself over to the hang glider and to your surprise it folds out quickly, though you have to keep it in the right direction to stop the wind from blowing off the sails and from it shooting off without you. You strap yourself in and manage to get yourself away from the other falling debris.

Tipping the glider up lets you continue to fall, and just tipping the nose quickly slows you down with wind resistance. You keep working on slowing down until all the falling bits have fallen well beyond you. Then you slowly (but not too slowly) tip the glider up to catch the upwind.

Wham, you are thrown into the current and the glider creaks and bends. Nevertheless, you have just enough control of the machine to sail, at least a bit. Having never flown a hang glider before you are very careful not to let it stall (to stall means to turn it so that it would fall from the sky). But try as you might, the glider continues to stall and before long you are falling helplessly out of control into the earth. You hit the earth with mortal force. Go to Option D5.

Option D5

You failed to make a decision that saved you from the whim of fate. Better luck next time. Game over.

Did you succeed? Did you choose the right option? Before you read on here, go back and read all the options you didn't choose.

Read on below only after reading all the options.

Story debriefing: So, you think that this story is not fair, you feel cheated. Correct. There is *no* way to save yourself. Your cleverness cannot save you because in this story there is no tomorrow. Sometimes in life there is no happy ending.

13 Uncertainty

This story is about great uncertainty, and about the ultimate poverty of induction on which we base our taken for granted world.

"Can I be sure that you will be here when I get back from school, Mummy?" asked Angus.

"Why of course you can be sure Angus," replied his mother.

"But, Mummy, how *can* I be sure?" inquired Angus.

"Well dear, I am here cleaning house, and when you get back from school, I will have cleaned the house, been to work and have come home to be here for you when you return."

"Mummy, how can you be sure that you will be here. It seems that you hope you will be here when I return, even that you intend to be here when I return, but can you be sure?"

"Darling, wherever do you come up with these things?"

"I don't know Mummy; my teacher says I think too much."

"Well, that can't be a bad thing can it - fancy a teacher saying that most of my teachers told me that I didn't think enough!"

"Mummy, you still haven't answered my question. Can you be sure?"

"Darling, I will do everything in my power to make sure that I am here for you, but I can't actually guarantee it. Have I ever not been here for you?"

"No - you have always been there, that is comforting, but because you have always done something or always managed to achieve something, does that mean that it will happen again?

Could it not be that you are overdue for failing to do what you expect, perhaps your being here every afternoon is against all the odds, and perhaps it will never happen again?"

"Darling, sometimes you *do* think too much."

Angus was starting to get a little agitated. "Mummy, that means that because you are here today, it doesn't mean that you will be here tomorrow. The sky may not be blue, the ground may not be solid, we may not be able to breathe air, white may be black, old may be new, good may be bad. Mummy, how can we be certain? It may be that we are all doomed."

"Darling, we may have all been doomed yesterday, but we are here today to eat breakfast, to brush our teeth, and to enjoy the sunshine. White is white, black is black, good is good, bad is bad."

"But Mummy, how can we be certain?"

"Darling, it is not possible ever to be certain of anything."

"Mummy, does this mean that I should not even be certain that I am here, or that you are there or that we are eating breakfast? Could it all be an illusion?"

"It could my dear."

"Then how do I know that I am not alone? if I am not certain of not being alone then I might as well be alone. How do people live without certainty, Mummy? How do they live without knowing about tomorrow, isn't it all too frightening, too dangerous, and too lonely?"

"Darling, if we were to live our lives in fear of uncertainty, it would be no life. If we would live our life with total certainty, then life would have no meaning. The meaning of our lives comes from the balance of certainty. How much would we value something if we knew we would live forever and that we would have everything just as it was, forever."

"Perhaps, Mummy, it's just easier to accept things the way they seem to be. Perhaps, just perhaps that's the way things are. But then again, perhaps, just perhaps, it's not."

14 A Dog's Day

This is a story about emptiness and fulfilment. The story addresses the way that the individual can lose sight of direction and how, through the association with others they can achieve self-respect and assist in the self-respect of others. The story helps readers to recognise the value in human relationships.

Growing up for me was a bit hard. I guess it was probably a bit hard for my mum too and for my dad. My brother probably also had a hard time of it, not to mention the dog.

My teachers had it rough, though probably most of them deserved it. There were the people next door, on both sides and the people out the back. I gave them a hard time. Then there was Gronk who owned the shop on the corner. I gave him a hard time. Then the people with the pink house and my grandparents and their dog, and the people who lived next to them and their dogs.

There was Mrs Truro who lived round the corner and her dog. Looking back on it now, I had a real thing about dogs. There was the guy with the red nose at the supermarket, he didn't have it good with me and then there was the postman, the guy who came around with the soft drinks, Mum's friend Trish and her family, their dog and their next-door neighbours and their dogs. There was Carl and his dog, Mary and Jon and their son and dog, and Barry and Sue and their dog - none of them had it good. Very few people who I met had it good, with me anyway. I was the common element and so I guess I was probably responsible. For a girl I was a big handful, or so my parents used to say.

I know it sounds odd, but I never felt that I was me when I was a young girl. I felt I must have been someone else. Perhaps I had been switched in hospital at birth by an untrustworthy doctor who knew that the rich parents who had a scrawny brat like me could really do with a bouncing rosy-cheeked baby girl. I was always scrawny and pimply, right since I was born - I am sure of it. Perhaps I did the rounds in the hospital being swapped from parents to parents until some unsuspecting parents were given me because there was no one else to swap with.

In my bedroom, when I wasn't out playing with one of the dogs, I would stare up at the ceiling. The ceiling had patterns on it, and I had sailed over them a thousand thousand times wishing I were someone else, but exactly who I really didn't know.

Six o'clock came and it was time for tea. As was often the case I had been grounded and confined to my room for riding my bike over Tanny's tail. Anyway, it wasn't my fault because he just wouldn't cooperate when I tried to put him in the basket of my bike so he could experience the joys of bike jumps. I went downstairs, had what I wanted of my tea - I *hate* casseroles, who ever invented them? - and I went to watch TV.

"Have you done your homework, Maggie?" asked Mum.

"I didn't have any, I finished it at school," I grunted in a sort of angry tone which meant to say, 'Just leave me alone.'
 "Can I go over to Trish's place?" I whined.

"Anything to get you out of here," she said, "and make sure you leave Hudson alone."

"Always do Mum, Hudson's *such a lovely* dog."

"Be back before eight," she said because parents must have to have the last say and for some reason always think they're going to get it.

"I can't hear you," I screeched as I tore out the door, "tell me when I get back," I sneered because parents need to know that they're not allowed to have the last say – it's a rule of growing up.

To get to Trish's place I had to go out the back fence through Mr Robson's place and say 'hello' to his dog - a silly great Labrador - it would lick a burglar I'm sure - then across the road past Mrs Truro's place (her dog goes crazy when you clink the gate) and up Wallace Road about five houses. Mrs Truro was a recluse, an old lady who since her husband died rarely left the house. I had seen her a few times at her door, sometimes coming out to see what had made her dog bark.

It was a cool night, and the breeze was blowing off the ocean. You could smell the sea and feel the salt even though from where I was, I couldn't quite see the water. I went up to the door and choosing not to press the button called out, "Trish."

There was no answer, so I went around the back.

"Shut up you stupid mut. Now, who's a little bog breath, sewer creeper then Hudson, you thicko, brainless poor excuse for a dog," I said as I looked dolefully into its eyes. At least that stopped the stupid thing from barking. I walked right around the house but there was no sign of activity. Trish was out. I was tempted to play catch the basketball with the dog, a game which had the odds stacked in favour of me I know, but as Hudson was as big as a house, I thought that evened it out a bit. But I didn't feel like doing that and so after I put the dog's dinner on the other side of the fence, just out of reach of its paw (Hudson had been putting on an alarming amount of weight and it's sometimes necessary to be cruel to be kind) I decided to take a stroll along the cliffs. Perhaps there would be some strays.

Walking to the cliffs took about ten minutes. It was now 6.30pm. Mum said, not that I heard her, to be back at 8pm. That means 8.15pm would be safe with a small excuse. If I hadn't already been in trouble, I could have got away with 9pm with a big explanation and a big effort to change the subject when she was about to impose her sentence. I reckoned that given the circumstances of the day with a bit of an excuse and a 'commitment to being good in the future,' I could comfortably get away with 8.30. Now, what was the excuse? ... Brilliant, I thought as I stumbled upon the perfect plan. As Trish was away, I had decided to walk Hudson, thus doing Trish a favour and Hudson a favour! I could return late, have an alibi (I could leave a note for Trish) be seen to have made up with the dog and I could return a hero and still be late. Now how was that a stroke of genius.

I trotted back up the street, wrote Trish a note, got Hudson's lead, opened the gate, walked him straight past his dinner, which I kicked back inside to hide the evidence and strutted off for the cliffs.

The sea was heaving and falling like the chest of a great sleeping giant. From a block away I could hear the enormous force of the sea smashing against the rock platforms below. As I drew closer, I could even hear the seething of the water as the waves retreated waiting for the next onslaught. It was cool and refreshing in that kind of spring way, after a nice clear day it left the evening cool and crisp.

Along the top of the cliffs was a line of parks which sometimes led straight to the cliffs and sometimes were fenced off. At one part there was a tremendous view of the coast, and through an eroded plinth it was possible to sit on the bench and watch the sea assaulting the shore. I pulled Hudson along towards the bench, but the noise was making him worried and besides he hated the sea - this was a good opportunity for me to help him confront his fears. "Stupid dog, it's only the sea."

"Damn," I cursed to myself as I neared the bench, for as I got closer, I could see that there was someone else there and I hadn't come here to have a chat. They wouldn't stay long once I got there, I assured myself.

As I neared the bench, I could see that it was a little old lady and as I drew very close, I could see that it was Mrs Truro. I now realised why the curtains hadn't moved when I clinked the gate when I passed her house; Mrs Truro had been here.

"Mrs Truro, what are you doing here?" I said in an upfront and slightly offensive way.

"I should think I'm doing much the same thing as you are, child," she said in a stern but kind of detached voice. "I'm look'n at the sea."

"Why are you *look'n* at the sea? Mrs Truro," I asked now trying to get rid of her.

"In 1963 my husband Barney and me we used to come up here, you know. Every Friday we'd get fish and chips from the shop over there, and we'd bring up some bread and butter and make chip butties. We'd cut each other slices of cheese too and we'd watch the sea. It's just the same as it was, child. The sea it never changes."

"But what are you doing here, now? Mrs Truro. I've not seen you out before. Should you be out this late in the cold?"

"I ain't been out much before. It's been three months since I've even been out of me house."

"Where do you get your food from then?" I asked because it seemed quite odd.

"The grocer drops me things off, I phone 'im and he drops 'em round, I don't cook now really. I live off cans of tuna, bread, tea, and cigarettes!"

"So Mrs Truro, you still haven't really told me why you're here?" I reminded her.
"Well child, I wanted to see the sea again. I wanted to smell the salt and sit here and remember the chip butties. I wanted to gaze out over the horizon and remember what happened here. Why exactly are you here, child?"

"I'm walking this dog."

"I'm glad to see that you like dogs, I've got a dog, it's a godsend really. He's my only friend. He's the only one on the planet now who knows anything about me. You see I tell him everything. It's a bit silly really, but that dog is a real friend to me. What's your name anyway?"

"Maggie"

"Maggie, there's one of the most awful things in life is being lonely. But I'm glad I've got me dog."

I don't exactly know what came over me, but I was struck, as if from nowhere, to make a generous gesture. It was perhaps the other me speaking, the one that I never really knew. "Mrs Truro, if I go and get some chips from the chip shop would you like some?"

"Chips 'eh, I haven't had chips for, let me see, almost twenty-five years," she stuttered, "twenty-five years," she began to laugh. "Isn't that funny, Maggie, twenty-five years and I haven't had any chips. Not one. I've forgotten what they taste like."

"I'll go and get some, Mrs Truro, just you wait here. Oh, would you look after Hudson?" I said as I looped his chain over the corner of the bench.

"When I got back Mrs Truro was there chatting wildly to the dog, who had done perhaps the most sensible thing it had yet done and had fallen asleep."

"You know Maggie, twenty-five years is a long time to have not had chips, I could be the only one alive in England who hasn't had a chip in twenty-five years."

"What have you been doing for twenty-five years Mrs Truro?

"Well since Barney died, I just stayed at home. At first some of his mates would come round, but that all stopped. Barney and I was such great mates. I really couldn't face it all when he died. Here I am now eighty-three and I haven't had chips for twenty-five years."

"Can I make you a chip buttie Mrs Truro?" I asked.

"Thank you," she replied. "I loved Barney so much. I was glad when Trumper came by, 'bout six years back. He was just a stray that came and never left. I feed him better than myself, I couldn't bear it if he left. He's the only thing that I care about now. You know Maggie, yours is the only kindness that I can remember receiving from anyone since Barney left and aside from Trumper of course. It's nice to have someone be kind to you."

"Thanks Mrs Truro, it's nice to be kind to someone."

"Maggie, I came out here because I've not been well and…" she broke off rather suddenly, and well anyway I wanted to see the sea. And, and… well … aren't these chips good. Twenty-five years," she said again as she gave a little chuckle.

We chatted for a while about how the town had changed. How people were different now and how the houses had changed and how rich people had started buying homes to visit just on the weekends and during the Summer, and how the place was now often deserted.

Eventually I saw the time and it was late, or at least later than I had expected, and I said goodbye to Mrs Truro and went home.

"Thank you, Maggie," she said. You don't know how much I've enjoyed our little chat and thank you so much for the chips."

"It's a pleasure Mrs Truro," I said as I grabbed Hudson roughly and went to go.

"Sometime you might like to look after my dog Maggie," she said, curiously, as I left.

"Sure thing Mrs Truro," I said not knowing exactly why, and knowing that if she knew that it was me who clinked her gate every other day and made her darling dog go crazy, it's the last thing she would have said.

I took Hudson back to Trish's place, and Trish had already returned, and she was delighted that I had been and walked the dog.

"That's not like you," she said.

"Oh, I love Hudson so so much," I replied in a sarcastic tone.

"Well anyway thanks for taking him, I rang your mother and let her know what was happening. She's expecting you home any minute now." I walked back through the gate and kicked the dinner bowl back outside.

"See ya Trish," I called as I went out the gate, back past Mrs Truro's place. I resisted the temptation to clink the gate, and back through Mr Robson's place and home. Mum didn't even bat an eyelid.

"Night Mum," I called into the sitting room.

"Goodnight, Maggie, don't forget your teeth," she called out to me as I walked past the bathroom.

"'Course not Mum."

That night I slept well enough, happy that I had done a good turn for an old lady and that perhaps I was beginning to be me after all.

That following week I was walking up to Trish's, and I saw an ambulance outside Mrs Truro's place. I asked the driver what had happened, and he said that Mrs Truro had died in her house and that the neighbours started being suspicious when the dog started behaving oddly. When they went in, they found her dead. They say she must have died in her sleep late in the night. The funny thing was, they said, that after having been a crabby old lady for as long as anyone remembered, she looked, kind of happy.

I was a bit shocked, in fact I was very shocked. I had no idea that she was, well, going to die.

I backed away from the ambulance and looked up the street. Instead of going to Trish's place I went back to the bench. When I walked around the corner, I could see the bench in the distance. I wandered over there to have a bit of a think.

'She must have known that it was going to happen,' I thought to myself. 'She knew that she was going, otherwise why would she have walked all the way here to the cliffs.' I realised that it must have been a great effort for her to get there because she was very frail. I thought it funny that I hadn't even thought of that at the time or how she would have got back home. She must have made it. I wondered whether the walk had killed her.

Then another great thought dawned upon me, 'What about Trumper?' Even though she was a stray years ago, Mrs Truro would have been horrified to think that he would be cast out. And besides he knew too much about her.

Deep down I knew that my dislike for dogs was in some way not real, and I knew that I had to look after Trumper for Mrs Truro. No one else would and it would be awful to take him to the pound.

As it happened, I collected Trumper and looked after him for four years until he died. I never felt the need to mistreat a dog again and even though Mrs Truro thought I did her a favour in her last moments; I think it was she that did me the good turn.

15 Butterfly Wings

This story is about cause and effect. The story looks at a chain of events and asks the question 'who is responsible?'

On Tuesday 27th September, Hong Li, who lived in a little agricultural village just outside of the bustling city Shantou, on the South-eastern coast of China, saw a butterfly where she had never seen a butterfly before. She saw the butterfly in the oddest of places, it had been attracted to a drainage outlet that poured waste from a factory into the river. He watched as a brightly coloured blue butterfly flapped its wings and drank the water from the drainage outlet. The little butterfly flapped its way along the riverbank, much as butterflies normally do, it was oblivious to the impact that it was about to have on so many things. Hong thought nothing much of what he saw, but this butterfly was to have serious implications.

When Hong went to school that day, he was asked by his teacher to choose something beautiful to write about. Hong wrote about the blue butterfly. When his teacher read his work and looked at his beautiful picture, she put it up on the notice board in the hallway.

Later, after school had finished, Xiao Chan came by. Xiao Chan cleaned the school. Although he could not read, he saw Hong Li's picture of the butterfly and he took a moment to admire it. The picture made him smile. Xiao Chan continued to clean the school, and when he left for the day, he didn't think any more about the butterfly.

The next morning Xiao went to work, this time in an office he also cleaned. Xiao cleaned the office of the 1st Porcelain Factory in the outskirts of Shantou. He cleaned the office early in the morning. When he was in the office, he saw on a desk a beautiful porcelain tea service. It was a new design that the company was considering manufacturing. Although he knew he shouldn't look, he picked up one of the cups in the set. As it was still not very light, he took the cup to the window in order that he might see it more clearly.

The cup attracted him because it had the same blue colouring as the picture of the butterfly that he had seen the day before. When he went to put the cup back on the desk, he tripped on the cord of the vacuum cleaner, and he fell and smashed the cup. Xiao told his supervisor about the breakage - sometimes these things happened and normally it didn't cause a problem. The breaking of the cup did not cause a problem for Xiao, well at least not one he could tell.

When Ju Lin came into work, he saw that the cup was broken and was angry. The cleaning supervisor had left a note, but Ju Lin's boss had asked him to send the cup to an embassy where it was to be a gift for a foreign diplomat. The set had to be sent that day and there was not time to make another. Although a blue set had been ordered Ju Lin had no alternative but to send a green set. Ju Lin was unhappy about this, but it was all he could do. The sending of the green set did not cause a problem for Ju Lin, well at least not one that he could tell.

Mr Wonju took receipt of the green tea set at the Emperor's Palace in Beijing. He had it carefully wrapped as a gift to the Austrian Trade Emissary Mr Schröder. Mr Schröder graciously received the set and thanked Mr Wonju for the set warmly. Although Mr Schröder had asked for a blue set, he agreed that a green one would do just as nicely. Mr Schröder did not expect that accepting the green tea set would cause any trouble.

When Mr Schröder showed the tea set to his wife, she was furious. "This is the third time you have brought me something that just doesn't go with the decor of our house. How many times do I have to tell you, blue, blue, blue." Mrs Schröder went to bed that night very cross. Mr Schröder, however, was used to his wife's bad temper and went to bed with a clear conscience and in fact even felt a little less guilty about his snoring that night.

The following morning after Mr Schröder went to work, Mrs Schröder, after she had had her shower, looked at the tea set once again which renewed her anger. She decided to go into the city and to buy a tea set that was the correct colour for her home. When she got into the car, she was furious, and she took less care with driving than she might otherwise have done. She sped into the city and took scant notice of the traffic signals. On the intersection of the Yushan Road and Yingchun Road, she collided with a big black car. No one was hurt, thankfully, but Mrs Schröder grew even angrier.

In the car was Gustav Jonsson who was going to the World Congress on Tropical Rainforest Clearing, which curiously was being held in London. It was a curious place to have a rainforest clearing conference because there is no tropical rainforest anywhere near London. In any case, the delay caused by the accident with Mrs Schröder meant that Mr Jonsson was unable to give his lecture on why an area of rainforest in Belize was not to be cut down. Although he sent a copy of the lecture to those with whom he had hoped to meet, being unable to explain himself about the rainforest led to a vote against the logging failing by just one vote, and the loggers would now proceed to destroy the forest. As a result, it was not possible to stop the loggers moving into the Belizean forest in the following week.

The logging of the rainforest near Corozal left many of the local people without the resources on which they had lived in the past. José Belas at once needed to seek a job in the city and so moved to Belmopan where he tried to find work to feed his family. Because he now had no way to earn a living without reason and without warning, he was forced to steal food for himself and for his family, until he could find work. Unfortunately for José, he was caught in the act of stealing fruit and was jailed without any consideration of what had happened to him. When he was in court a Mr Robert Bruce happened to be passing by, a reporter from the New York Times. He sat and watched the court case of José Belas whilst he was waiting to watch an important trial. Mr Bruce was touched by the story of Mr Belas even though he did not think about it again until he returned to New York.

Back in New York Mr Bruce returned to his office and was greeted by his secretary. He told her about what he had seen in Belize, and he told her as much as he knew of José Belas. He explained to her how he had been touched by his story. Joan Baldwin knew nothing of Belize and was quite intrigued and so during her lunch hour she went to the bookshop and looked for books on Central America. When she found the geography section, she picked up a book and beneath it was a book about international clothing designs which she left uncovered.

Xiao Ping, who was in the shop buying a copy of the Asian Wall Street Journal, happened to see the book that Mrs Baldwin had revealed and went over to look at it. He leafed through the book and decided that it would be a good gift for a friend and so he bought it. He collected his paper and the book and headed for the door, to catch a cab to the airport from where he was returning to China.

On returning to Guangzhou, Mr Ping posted the book to his friend Den Wong in Shantou who owned a company near to the river. When he opened the book, he looked through its pages and became inspired by what he saw. Den decided to open the factory early that day so that he could get started on some new ideas for designs he had got from the book. He opened the factory door, turned on the lights and drained the colour vats, as had to be done every morning.

The vats spilled their inks and resins into the drain which made their way out into the river and, just as that happened, another brightly coloured butterfly sprang out from the drainpipe just by where Hong Li lived.

Continuous Blinking

A whole bunch of things to think about...

1 Millfield Library

1. Where do history books belong in the library? With which other books?

2. Is history true?

3. What is the *truth* that Mrs Jacques is talking of in the latter part of the story?

4. How does fact gradually turn into fiction with the passage of time? Does this always happen? Is it a bad thing that this happens? Should people try to stop it happening?

5. Mrs Jacques runs a library in which it is hard to find a book. How might differently organised books in a library be useful? Could books be organised in more useful ways?

6. Do human beings normally like to organise the things they know? How do you store information in your mind – is it organised or disorganised? Why do we organise things?

7. Who decides whether something is properly organised or not? Could two libraries, having the same books but organised differently, be each as good as the other whilst being wholly different in terms of organisation?

8. Was André right to question Mrs Jacques, even though she was the librarian, and it was her decision how the library should be organised? Is it right to question things that have always seemed to be the same? Why is it sometimes difficult to judge things that have always been the way they are?

Something to do:

a. Imagine you were Mrs Jacques, write a paragraph arguing for the way she organised the library.

2 Gravity Hiccups

1. What would the world need to be like if precautions needed to be taken against gravity hiccups? What would have to change?

2. For most people, things day to day are fairly stable, however for others, enormous changes occur, sometimes in a very short period of time. Think of people or peoples who have had to cope with enormous and sudden change.

3. How do you think the human race would cope if something like gravity hiccups existed. How would the developed world cope and how would the less developed world cope?

4. Can you think of any events that have changed the world so suddenly and so significantly?

5. How would society help those people who had difficulty in coping with a changed situation?

6. The changes that would occur with gravity hiccups would mean that new things would need to be designed so human beings could do what they normally did. What things would become dangerous, what things would become impossible and what new things might it now be possible to do?

Something to do:

a. Make a design of modifications that would have to be done to either the classroom or one of the rooms in your home, for it to be safe from gravity hiccups.

3 The Dangers of Words

1. What would the signs have meant if both sides had said? "The statement on the other side of the mat is false."

2. If there were a mat that said on both sides, "The statement on the other side of the mat is true" could it be true that both statements were in fact lies?

3. How do we learn what things make sense? Do people have a better understanding of what 'makes sense' as they get older? Why or why not?

4. Can you think of any things in our world or society that are contradictions?

5. How do human beings cope with contradictions?

6. Is it possible to hold two opposing ideas in your mind at the same time?

7. Could the following statements all be true together? 'I like apples more than oranges.' 'I like oranges more than bananas.' 'I like bananas more than apples.' If so, how?

8. Why is it that a journey back from somewhere seems to take less time than it takes to get there?

9. How can we determine what is true or not when we read things?

Something to do:

a. Make a sign that contradicts itself.

4 The Trees

1. Why did Jack's soul never dance?

2. What does it mean for one's soul to dance?

3. Who are the people who live in our society whose souls never have an opportunity to dance?

4. Are there parts of you that fear to dance and show themselves? How do other people who have those talents and interests show themselves?

5. Was Jack's life one that was tragic?

6. What sorts of things do you keep secret?

7. What is the point of keeping a secret?

8. Is it noble to be able to keep a secret?

9. Are there times when a secret must not be kept?

10. Why are there national secrets?

11. How do countries deal with shame?

12. Is a shameful secret different from other secrets?

Something to do:

a. Make a poster that celebrates all the things that delight you. Don't just write football, skiing etc, but write sentences that define the *exact moment* which makes you really excited about what you are doing. On a piece of card draw a quick sketch of your face and write sentences defining these moments in rays extending from your face outwards from the centre.

5 Anstead

1. How were Anstead's actions unhelpful?

2. How were Anstead's actions helpful?

3. What is the implication for truth when the truths on which they are based are mixed with error or falsehoods?

4. Is it a bad thing that what we regard as true may be wrong?

5. Are there any times when errors in the way we understand history might be a good thing?

6. How easy is it for history to be wrong?

7. Who decides what the 'real' history is?

8. Can there be two or more acceptable histories at the same time. Consider the idea of creation and that of evolution.

9. In whose interests is it that history may be wrongly recorded?

10. How could you go about ensuring that history was wrongly recorded?

11. Is there a real truth, or does what is true change as the human race changes?

Something to do:

a.   From your class/group, or with another person find an issue about which there is some form of very minor disagreement. Maybe which is the best colour. Hold a mock court or hearing to try to ascertain the truth. At the end of the hearing, discuss how people's understanding of the facts were at variance with one another.

6 Florian, for want of a better name

1. If Florian knew the risks, should he have explored the bathroom?

2. How do we decide what an acceptable amount of danger is? Crossing the road is dangerous, but we still do it - why do we expose ourselves to danger and how do we decide what is too dangerous?

3. Think of some people who have lived dangerous lives and who have died. Should they not have lived so dangerously? Did they do the right thing in living as they did?

4. This story does not have a happy ending. How many stories can you think of that do not end on a happy note? Do stories have to end on a happy note? Do episodes in life always end on a happy note?

5. The story has a sudden ending. When do episodes in life have sudden endings? How do human beings cope with their own sudden endings or the sudden endings of other things, or other people?

Something to do:

a.   Make a list of dangerous things you have done. Make a scale of danger from 1-10 with 1 being the least dangerous thing you do or have done, and 10 being the most dangerous thing you do or have done. Each point on the scale may have more than one action.

7 Renata

1. Our senses sometimes give us the wrong information. Consider for example, optical illusions. Our eyes tell us something we might know is not the case. How can we tell that our senses are not perpetually fooling us? Is it possible that they are fooling us more than we think? Is it possible that we are nothing like what we appear to look like?

2. Was Renata right, when she decided that she must exist because she was thinking? Is it possible to not exist if you are thinking?

3. Consider the statement: 'some thinking is going on; I wonder if it's me?' What sort of sense does this statement make?

4. How do human beings cope with the fact that things may not be as they seem to be? How do we cope with the fact that, although unlikely, reading the next question on this page, would cause the end of the universe? Or the possibility that going to school may, in fact, not be good for you?

5. How does it feel when you find out something you long thought to be true is really false. What if most things were false? What if everything was

illusory? Would it matter? If you knew everything was illusory, how would it change your life?

6. What does it mean at the end of the story when Renata says that she still had to rescue everything else? How could it be, that after doubting her own existence, there could be doubt about the existence of everything else?

Something to do:

a. Make a list of five things you 'know' to be true. Work on these 'truths' and work out exactly how you know them to be true. At each stage ask the question, "Is there any way that this could be false?"

8 The World Department Store

1. Cosmo is attracted to the World Department Store by the bargains. Is cost the best way to determine whether you should buy something?

2. If something you want to buy is a good product and a good price, what other things might make you reluctant to buy it?

3. Should we buy things that are made under conditions of which we would not approve?

4. How can we tell if a product has been manufactured using child labour or even slavery?

5. If we buy a product that is manufactured by means of which we don't approve, are we personally responsible for providing a market for products produced in this way, and are we then responsible for the treatment of workers in factories so far away?

6. If people always want to buy the cheapest goods, what does this do to for people living in less well-off countries?

7. When we pick up things that we already own, do we ever consider, for a moment the lives of the people who manufactured them?

8. When you purchase an expensive brand-named item, how much money goes to the company and how much to the person who spent time making the product?

9. Is this system of manufacturing and commerce ethical? Why or why not? If it is not ethical, how could it be made to be ethical? What would be the challenges of doing this?

10. Is it possible to drive change by buying ethical products? Would this just mean that someone else would buy the unethical product? If a company were to improve how it made a product, it might make less profit or not sell goods because they had become more expensive. This might mean they may go out of business. Maybe only the cheaper goods made from unethical products will be made and bought. How can this be avoided?

11. Once Cosmo had been made aware of the conditions under which the things in his room

were made, do you think it made him feel a little uneasy about them?

12. How many items with which we are surrounded might you think it reasonable to feel uneasy about?

Something to do:

a. Explore brand names you are most enthusiastic about on the internet to find out how ethical their manufacturing processes are. Compare what they say on their own websites with comments made from outside the company. Research 'slavery,' and 'child labour,' to find out what kinds of products are made under these conditions.

9 Ermonza

1. What does it mean to retreat into your own world?

2. How often do you go and spend time alone? Do you like being alone? Why or why not?

3. Do you have a place to go when you want to think? If so, where is it and why do you like to go there?

4. How do you cope when you are angry? How do you cope when you are angry, and you feel you are right? How do you cope when you are angry, and you know that you are in the wrong? Are you ever in the wrong?

5. Do you ever consider what other people might think of how you act when you are cross?

6. Think about how other people are when they are cross. Make a list of ways that people get cross.

7. Do you ever enjoy feeling sorry for yourself? How do you snap yourself out of it?

8. How is it that we carry our parents and family around us inside our heads? Have you ever noticed a brother or sister do something that is just the way Mum or Dad does something? Have you ever noticed yourself doing something and feeling, 'I feel like my mother or father' doing that?

9. How does hard physical activity make you feel better when you have been cross?

10. Do you always follow your conscience?

11. Why is it sometimes hard to do seek conciliation or agreement when you have been cross?

Some things to do:

a. Make a list of ways that people deal with their anger in a positive way. Think of private and public examples and include these on your list. You don't have to give examples, but you could classify types of responses. Think about anger that has led to violence and ask how anger could have been more effectively dealt with. You might do this individually or you might work on this as a whole class project.

10 Mrs McCulvert Lived Alone

1. Why do older people sometimes live a life of isolation?

2. How do people allow themselves to become lonely?

3. Why do people collect things?

4. When was the last time that you had a really good conversation with someone? Were you expecting it, or did it just happen. Did the conversation include anything surprising?

5. Have you ever made the effort to have a conversation with someone who needed company, just because you thought they might be lonely?

6. By her own admission Mrs McCulvert had led a lonely life. How much did William's contribution make amends? Is it possible for a whole life to be improved all at once, even at the end of one's life? How would it be if Mrs McCulvert had not managed to talk with William before she died?

7. There was nothing much to gain for William in his helping Mrs McCulvert. If he did it just to be kind, what is it to be kind? Why do we do things just to be kind? Is this a sensible way to behave? If so, then why?

8. What does it mean to die peacefully? How can it be that people don't die peacefully. Can someone die a violent death and yet die peacefully and someone else die a quiet but restless death?

9. Mrs McCulvert was able to die peacefully. In order to do this, she managed to 'get her house in order,' which means that before she died, she sorted out some of the things that had been worrying her for many years. Do some people keep their houses in better order than others? How do they do that? How can someone let their house get out of order?

10. What happens to all our belongings when we die. Some may be passed on to other members of a family, but so many of the things about which we have a story to tell become junk. When you buy antique furniture or things that are second hand,

to what extent are the stories of these objects

contained within them?

Some things to do:

a. Look at something second hand and ruminate on the stories that could be told about the previous owner.

b. Listen to the Beatles' song Eleanor Rigby. Make a poster suggesting ways that people could try to reduce the loneliness budget in our society. Organise a pledge from everyone in the class that all will telephone a relative or long-lost friend within a week. Report back.

11 André and the Toaster

1. What problem did André have with the designs of the toasters when he went into the electrical shop?

2. Should appliances *look like* what they *do*? Should you be able to look at an appliance and tell what it does, or should design be used to disguise it? Things of some things that seem to hide what they do. Is this good design?

3. Consider the design on some of the electronic items you use. Consider particularly the design of mobile phones, game consoles, cars etc. What shapes do they have? Why?

4. Sometimes design makes an appliance easier to use, and at other times it makes it more interesting to look at. Consider examples of these two design ideas and come up with examples of efficient and inefficient design. Also look for good aesthetic design and poor aesthetic design.

5. Have you ever been frustrated by the design of something? For example, you may have found it unnecessarily complicated to program a machine or to operate a camera. Why was it difficult to complete the task you set out to do?

6. Have you ever seen or been given an object for which you could not work out its purpose or function?

Some things to do:

a. Create an award that may be given to things in your school that are well designed. Look out for projects, buildings, timetables, virtually anything. You might want to have a design week and focus on things that are well put together in your school. You might also want to award a 'wooden spoon' award, for the thing at use in school that is the least well designed or thought out.

b. Look at some products and their instruction books. Evaluate them for their good design and straightforward explanation. Write to the companies commending good design and criticising poor design.

12 Inevitability

1. This story is about inevitability or fate. What does it mean for something to be inevitable? What does it mean when someone asks the question, 'do you believe in fate?'

2. Are the decisions we make planned out, or is it just a matter of what is going to happen, unfolding? Does a greater being know what decisions we are going to make before we make them?

3. If a greater being does know what decisions we are going to make, does that mean that we really can't make decisions or make a real choice?

4. Who provides us with the choices we must make in life?

5. How do we make decisions about the choices we have to make? Do we always choose rationally or wisely?

6. Consider some of the decisions that important people have made, consider recent events in

politics or public life. Can you see anyone who might have regretted the decisions they have made?

7. Does believing in fate make people lethargic and uninterested in life?

Some things to do:

a. Construct a maze that has no entrance and no exit. Make a poster with a caption that makes people think about this issue.

b. Look at the website www.despair.com and think about what role their products have in society? Make paired posters with a motivating theme and a demotivating theme. Which is true?

(Beware: this is a kind of joke website, selling funny posters, but it plays on personal fears. Don't take it too seriously, seriously!)

13 Uncertainty

1. Angus is concerned about whether his mother will be at home when he returns from school. Is this a reasonable fear?

2. What do you think Angus fears?

3. If the fear Angus has about the disappearance of his mother is reasonable, then how can he go on with his life? It is certain, given the dangers of modern life, that there is a chance that his mother will not be there on his return.

4. How do we cope with the everyday fear that we may be abandoned, in one way or another, by the people who we believe love us?

5. How can we be certain that our lives are as we perceive them to be?

6. Can we be certain that the whole earth was not created five minutes ago, with every person on it having a set of ideas and memories that just happen to relate to each other's?

7. Have you ever had an experience that made you think that something was not quite what you thought it was? Have you for example ever had an experience of déjà vu, where you recollect having done something before even though, as far as you can remember, you have not?

8. If you think about these things from time to time, why is it that these fears don't become ever present, paralysing us with fear in all that we do?

Something to do:

a. Make a list of those things that could happen to us during the lesson, during the day, during the course of a week. Consider your knowledge of current affairs to ask which events like this have occurred to other people. How do we live managing these fears?

14 A Dog's Day

1. Why was Maggie's life so directionless? How might you know it was directionless?

2. What does it mean to have a directionless life?

3. Who do you know who has a directionless life?

4. What does it mean for a life to have direction?

5. Is it necessary to have a 'directed' life?

6. Does someone need to find a direction in their life?

7. Does someone sometimes have a direction in their life and at other times not?

8. If one wants to find a direction in life, how does one go about it?

9. Can other people provide you a direction in life?

10. Can some people go in the wrong direction in life?

11. Can people be heading in two directions at once?

12. Can some people spend their whole life going in the wrong direction?

13. How was Mrs Truro helped by Maggie?

14. How was Maggie helped by Mrs Truro?

15. Did Mrs Truro intend to help Maggie?

16. Did Maggie intend to help Mrs Truro?

17. Were both Mrs Truro and Maggie looking for help?

18. How did the short relationship between Maggie and Mrs Truro help them re-orientate themselves?

19. How do human relationships help people re-orientate themselves?

Some things to do:

a. Make a list of people who you know, try to ascertain in what directions their lives are heading.

b. Make an inventory of your own life and ask yourself in which directions you are heading.

c. Think about people or events that have made you think differently about something.

15 Butterfly Wings

1. Who was responsible for the chain of events that occurred in this story?

2. Were some people more responsible than others?

3. Was the chain of events caused by the butterfly, or by Mr Wong's emptying of the vats?

4. How much of what you do affects others?

5. Do you think you might have been responsible for a catastrophe you know nothing about? Would it be your fault?

6. Do good things happen because of bad things?

7. Do bad things happen because of good things?

8. If someone doesn't notice you doing something, can that something have consequences?

9. What is a consequence?

10. If one person does something as a result of another, how much is that action attributable to the doer and how much to the person who

provided the situation in which that action was likely?

11. Can a criminal be held responsible for his or her crimes?

12. How much crime can be attributable to poverty, poor education, depression etc?

13. To what extent are you responsible if someone reacts badly to something you do?

14. Do you believe in fate? What is the relationship between fate and this story?

Something to do:

a. Consider an action that you might take. It might be something very slight. Consider a chain of events that might occur because of something that you have done. The first step may be something that no one else notices.